Praise for Bragi Ólafsson

Bragi Ólafsson

Narrator

Translated from
the Icelandic by
Lytton Smith

OPEN LETTER
LITERARY TRANSLATIONS FROM THE UNIVERSITY OF ROCHESTER

First edition, 2018
All rights reserved

[Hello to Jason Isaacs]

Tristan Corbière line on pages 18 & 130 was originally translated by Michael Hamburger.

Library of Congress Cataloging-in-Publication Data: Available.
ISBN-13: 978-1-940953-82-3 / ISBN-10: 1-940953-82-0

This project is supported in part by an award from the New York State Council on the Arts with the support of Governor Andrew M. Cuomo and the New York State Legislature

This book has been translated with a financial support from

Printed on acid-free paper in the United States of America.

Text set in Janson, an old-style serif typeface named for Dutch punch-cutter and printer Anton Janson (1620–1687).

Design by N. J. Furl

Open Letter is the University of Rochester's nonprofit, literary translation press:
Dewey Hall 1-219, Box 278968, Rochester, NY 14627

www.openletterbooks.org

Narrator

Four friends have decided to spend a weekend together in a villa in Paris, with a view to eating themselves to death. Perhaps that's not what they set out to do, but it seems to be the underlying goal, and once they enter the house it takes over. They're middle-aged men, perhaps a bit older, called Ugo, Marcello, Michel, and Philippe. The house they're staying in is owned by Philippe's family: a beautiful, stately house, a sort of small mansion, somewhere outside the city center. Ugo is a restaurateur and chef. There's some tension between him and his wife: we get an insight into their feelings as we watch him sharpen his carving knives inside their restaurant before going to meet his companions; she, his wife, asks just what he is planning to do with all those knives this weekend. Philippe is a judge, unmarried, and lives with his old nanny, Nicole, who looked after him as a child and still seems to take care of all his needs, including those that, to her way of thinking, protect him from any desire to seek out the favors of other women. In other words, she coddles him. The third friend, Marcello, is played by Marcello Mastroianni. He is Italian, like Ugo; the others are French. He is an airline captain for Alitalia, a womanizer who has begun to worry deeply about his declining sexual prowess. The fourth is Michel, a television producer, divorced and tired of life. They are all rather handsome men, especially Marcello. They are elegantly dressed and sophisticated. Their refinement is especially evident when it comes to food. The day after they arrive at the villa they decide to hire some prostitutes, Marcello's idea. They only hire three women, however, because Philippe doesn't approve of the idea; he's mindful of what his old nanny would say. But at the very moment these gentlemen are organizing their liaison with the prostitutes, a group of schoolchildren shows up in front of the house, accompanied by their teacher, a handsome, plump woman whose role in the story, we can see at first glance, will obviously not be confined to that of school mistress. Her name is Andrea. One of the boys in the class is sent to knock on the front door and ask that the class be allowed in to see a certain tree in the garden, a linden with connections to the eighteenth-century French poet Boileau. At the conclusion of the class's visit, the aforementioned four gentlemen invite the children and their teacher in for some little hors d'oeuvres Ugo has prepared. And, following from that, the men invite Andrea to stay to dinner. She

accepts, and sits down to dine with them and the three prostitutes. Her visit stretches on until you might say that she's finally
become one of the group. In fact, she becomes the life and soul
of the place, the person who best appreciates the craft involved
in Ugo's food, and she is no less appreciative of the men who
have invited her in. Without any great preamble, Andrea and
Philippe decide to form a holy union. Yet she still gets into bed
with all four of them, and to that degree takes care of them far
better than the three prostitutes, who find things overly de-
bauched and make themselves scarce. The first of the four friends
to die is the pilot, Marcello. The night after they abandon ship—
the prostitutes, that is—he freezes to death in the open-top
Bugatti racing car he has been working on getting running in the
garage beside the house. It's a cold night—winter has arrived—
and his companions place his corpse in the kitchen, in a cold-
storage room with a window through which his closed eyes look
out at his surviving comrades. The next to go is Michel. His
death is no less figurative than Marcello's. He dies on the balcony, the one leading out into the garden from the living room.
Indeed, you could say the reason for Michel's unusual death is
that, from an early age, his stern mother forbid him from ever
passing gas when someone else might possibly hear. He confesses
this weakness to his companions once it becomes clear that he is
in the process of endangering his health. His mother's strict rules
have continued to govern him into adulthood, well into middle
age, which means he never lets himself release his inner pressure.
Even when it becomes a nuisance, and suppressing it becomes
very evident, especially compared to the way his friends deal with

the cornucopia of food and drink, which they're partaking of with the sole aim of getting the greatest amount possible into one's body. Marcello, for example, shamelessly allows himself to break wind at the dinner table, in front of Andrea and the prostitutes, but Michel gets up from the table and goes outside, where he expels so violently that it is, to put it mildly, uncomfortable to hear. And to see. As time passes, repeat incidents grow more painful, and it is difficult to imagine that it's possible to top them using the medium of film. In the wake of Marcello's death, it might be said that Michel's deflation is absolute. It happens as follows: the remaining four, Michel, Andrea, Ugo and Philippe, are gathered in the living room so that they can taste Ugo's latest concoctions and remember Marcello. A weight hangs over the group, though their appetite hasn't diminished. True, Michel has no desire for food; it isn't sitting well in his stomach. He goes to the piano and begins to play the song that resounds throughout the film, a theme of sorts. A song at once sensual and melancholy, a slow rumba beat, a song that's hard to dislike. Michel's playing does nothing to diminish that effect. But suddenly, as he sits at the piano wearing the late Marcello's white cardigan, a harsh sound escapes from him. In light of what has already happened, perhaps the sound doesn't strike the others as entirely surprising, but they are uncomfortable. Michel lifts himself up from his chair, trying to ease his discomfort, continuing to play the whole time. Soon the magnitude of sounds crescendos, and the others, who at first respond with nervous laughter, begin to find it rather alarming, and you imagine they fear their companion is about to float off into the air. The soothing melody begins to hasten on a trifle, to run ahead of itself. When the camera zooms in on Michel, standing at the piano, it shows sweat streaming down his face; it's obvious how much he's suffering, that he feels tremendous pain. He knows these are his last moments, that his body can't endure. Indeed, the song pauses. But the rumbling continues. Not for long, though. There's a deathly silence in the room. Michel turns around and looks desperately at his companions. Then he seeks out, almost involuntarily, the door to the balcony, heading toward the only fresh air available. When he steps outside, his feet keep him going for three or four steps, but then—and this happens very quickly—he dives forward, like he is swimming, and lands prostrate, his stomach across the balcony's wide railing. Right away, all strength leaves his body. Ugo, Philippe, and Andrea approach the door, terrified. These are pregnant moments, even, you might say, swollen; we hear dogs barking on the gravel drive in front of the house. Michel seesaws on the railing. His limbs jerk almost imperceptibly. And the barking of the dogs intensifies; they fully understand what's happening. When the camera pans back to Michel, the consequences of his tragic flatulence become apparent. His beige pants are now green. Philippe and Ugo take his hands and drag him back to be propped up against the balustrade pillars. They retreat to a safe distance inside, along with Andrea, and watch Michel from the doorway as he sits in a puddle of his own liquid feces. He inclines his head slightly forward; his hands, which are lying open-palmed on the concrete balcony, invite us to approach him. There is a tranquility to this image, though the dogs keep on barking. It's as if eternity itself has been captured on film. And yet it is here, at this moment in the cinema on Hverfisgata, that the thread of the film gets broken in the eyes of one particular moviegoer in the theater, a man who will shortly take over as narrator. Because he, the narrator, leaves the movie theater. Why? Because another person, someone the narrator has been pursuing all afternoon, from the post office on Austurstræti to the movie theater on Hverfisgata via stops at several other places, has got out of his seat and walked out of the room. This person couldn't take it any longer. The man's name is Aron Cesar. It took the narrator, however, a moment to decide whether he should continue to sit and watch the movie, or else follow Aron Cesar. He opted for the latter choice.

Five or Six Hours Earlier

He'd taken a number. He hadn't at first realized he needed to do so in order to get in line. And as he waited his turn, he wondered what words best describe the color of fire. Would you use yellow, or red? Orange? Blue? He had clapped eyes on a postcard featuring a picture of a volcanic eruption on the rack at the door to the post office, and though it was a color photograph, he couldn't decide what colors it showed; moreover, the eruption on the postcard brought other images of fire to mind. Or other metaphors. "Thirty-five," called a sales clerk. "Thirty-six," the other clerk called. But he was not number thirty-five or six. I'm *thirty-five years old*, he thinks, but it's not yet my turn. "Thirty-six?" the woman called again. "No one has thirty-six?" A little period of silence. "Thirty-seven?" Is there no number thirty-seven?

he thinks. The black woman standing behind him gives herself up. She's wearing a crisp, white, long dress, and he can imagine it will take on a different image once she goes out in the rain later; the shape will cling to the woman, making her outline clearer. From behind, he judges she is about thirty. When she turns around and beckons with her index finger, he momentarily thinks she's gesturing to him, but it soon becomes apparent she's addressing her child, a girl he estimates is six or seven. A young mother, he thinks. She will be forty years old when her daughter is fully grown. It must have significantly different effects on the personality of a child, he muses, to grow up with parents who are just under fifty when they give birth to a child compared, say, to growing up with people who are in their twenties. Worse, he expects, especially for an only child. To spend the first years of your life, and indeed all the years to date, as is his own case, in the home or, rather, the house of a man and a woman who are in no way prepared for having a child: that must mold the child in a rather decisive fashion. Not just must: does so, in reality. He is still thinking about himself. This young, dark-complexioned girl is not forced to listen to nineteenth-century violin sonatas over breakfast, he thinks. But how has that affected him? It is the nature of progeny to disturb existing forms, assuming, that is, the parents have some form or pattern to which they are trying to hold. What's more, in their eyes, it takes the child too long to develop into a comprehensive image with fixed form, he thinks, never mind a frame around the picture.

•

I think. G. thinks. The one I call G., because his name displeases
him, and always has. The one who is constantly thinking about
form and shape.

•

I'm still waiting for number 41 to be called up. I've finished
looking at the postcards on the stand across from the white cardboard boxes on the wall shelves to the left. They are different
sizes, but together they form a very beautiful whole, a family of
five boxes, each placed inside the other, the smallest into the next
smallest, and so on. The dark-skinned mother and daughter have
completed their errand, and leave the room. I follow them with
my eyes. But when I turn back toward the clerks, I notice a man
I know, or rather I know who he is. He stands a little way inside
the room, near the counter, somewhat obstructed by an elderly
woman. Strange to see this man here, I think. But what is so
strange about it? He's my contemporary, and although he for his
part has no idea who I am, or shouldn't have, I can say that I
know who he is all too well. More than once, more than twice,
I've wished this particular individual did not exist. Or, at least,
did not exist in the same space as me, at the same time, with
the same people. Of course, this was very foolish thinking, and it
was a while ago now. Back then, I even devised strategies to get
this man out of the way, take him off the board in some manner,
although the implementation of my plans never got beyond the
idea stage. But here he is, as I said. I have not seen him in a while.
And I have also not been contemplating him for long in the post

office when his phone rings. Apparently a busy man. The ring on his cell phone can hardly be called a ring; it is more like some kind of music, music with an obtrusive beat. As soon as he starts talking into the phone, he realizes it's his turn. As he walks up to the counter, still with the phone to his ear, I'm aware again of his peculiar gait, which I'd perpetually allowed to get on my nerves, time and again, because of the decided self-confidence it implied.

•

Perpetually. Decided. That's how G. phrases it. How he thinks. But it's unthinkable that this man, who has now surfaced here, all of a sudden, in the post office, has had such words pass through his head. *Decided* and *perpetually.* How did the line in the poem go? *In my distastes above all I have elegant tastes.*

•

Aron Cesar. He talks into the phone while he hands the clerk a letter, no, a small package. His voice is so low that G. cannot hear a single word of what he is saying. He sees that Aron is telling the woman something while pointing at the package. Unlikely that he's letting her know what's inside. The woman looks at him, half sullenly, while he pays for the shipment by credit card. Possibly he *was* informing her what was in the package. Why else would he have been pointing at it while saying something to the woman? But if he had been letting the woman know the contents, G. knows why: because he is lying about it. Aron switches off his phone and slips his card back into his wallet. When he turns around to go, his countenance more visible to G. than before, a certain period of G.'s life rushes through his mind, the years characterized by an imaginary battle with the man now standing in front of him. The boy, as he'd been then. And still is, no doubt. Amid the images flash speculations about the form I mentioned earlier, that strict form I have dedicated my life to, one way or another. In fact, it is this point in my life, which I connect to this man here in the post office in my memory, which is the only formless part. And as soon as I mention the word, I know that, compared to Aron Cesar, my own physical form is not as well-made as his. Or as well-maintained. Not as likely to capture the attention of those who constantly rove about with open eyes looking to be reassured that their normal shape is normal after all. When Aron sets off from the post office, it dawns on G. what his gait resembles. He is the walking pelican he once saw at the zoo in Paris.

•

But it is not just the unshakable certainty over his own excellence that leads Aron Cesar to move over the earth's surface this way. Thoughtlessness and stupidity also fill people with a sense of security. And while we're on the subject of thoughtlessness, that word must have a role in the snap decision G. takes to pursue Aron when he walks out of the post office. It is not until a minute or two later, when they are outside a different building on the other side of the street, that he realizes he is still holding his envelope in his hand. It takes him a whole minute to realize this must indicate his decision to go after Aron had been involuntary. He does not come to his senses until he runs his eyes over a book displayed on a table on the second floor of the bookstore opposite the post office, part of the so-called beach-reading sale. On the cover of the book is an image of a white mailing envelope with a blue-and-red striped border and the words *par avion* in one corner. Aron has, in other words, entered the bookshop opposite the post office. And G. follows behind, in from the rain which might well set Austurstræti afloat. It seems likely Aron will be here a while.

•

G. puts his envelope back into his bag.

•

It had taken him a moment or two to call the name to mind. G. had immediately remembered Cesar, but not Aron, not until he was contemplating him from behind the counter. Which is strange because, as I mentioned, this was the individual G. had had firmly in mind for a long time. But as he observes Aron at the magazine display inside the bookstore, his memory suggests that Aron is Óskarson, named after his mother, Ósk Völundardóttir. And G. knows the woman. Although he does not pay much attention to what happens inside the Icelandic Parliament, he knows Ósk Völundardóttir was a Member of Parliament for one or other of the parties, knowledge that has stuck in his memory, unlike other similar trivia, because at one time they had practically knocked each other over in the street in front of Parliament, G. and this woman. He was passing by one day a few years back, it was winter, he remembers that it was snowy and cold, and at the very moment he walked past the building she stormed out the front door, Ósk Völundardóttir, as if fleeing from something. And she collided with him. He remembers her apologizing. She took off so fast he felt sure she would get into another collision before getting to the other side of the square at Austurvöllur. He also remembers wondering whether he, rather than she, should not have apologized for getting in the way of a person who ran the country. But maybe she was hurrying some dirty laundry away from Parliament, and all her attention was concentrated on not spilling her bag. That her son, Aron Cesar, had lied about the contents of a package at the post office, as G. had watched him do, is not something plucked from thin air, some sick notion from a hypochondriac. Shortly before Sara and Aron split up, he had been convicted of a similar crime; it is not impossible he was committing the same crime again at the post office.

•

He considers hurrying back across the street with the envelope. He would be able to keep an eye on the entrance to the book-store from the window of the post office. But he could also nip in there sometime later; he has the whole day ahead of him.

•

But what had Sara been doing with this boy who was so obviously trouble? Sara's father was one of the most renowned composers in Iceland. Her mother, a violinist, was likewise well-known in the music world, though her fame came partly from playing her husband's works. I mention the parents because of the way I imagine Sara was raised, and how I see her upbringing: a stark contrast to the decision to throw her lot in with Aron Cesar, this half-Brazilian ne'er-do-well, a boy who appeared to have no other aim in life than playing a role, any role, in the underworld.

•

It so happens that as soon as G. thinks of the word *underworld* Aron goes down into what you could call the bookstore's underworld. After stopping a moment in the atrium by an advertising banner on the left, he descends to the basement, down a spiral staircase, to the children's books and toy section. G. decides to wait for him on the first floor. Aron is likely heading to the restroom, which G. knows is by the children's section. He loiters by the CDs along the wall to the right of the stairs, along past the stationery section, and examines among other things an elegant box of Schumann symphonies. Robert Schumann, who in the faster sections of his sonatas for violin and piano had keyed up the atmosphere of G.'s youth, of his mornings. It occurs to him that Sara would have enjoyed hearing about that misery. When he recalls the onset of one of Schumann's sonatas, one which is embedded in his mind like his own name, he thinks a story like this would have provoked Sara to laughter, to at least a smile, because it was surely recognizable from her own upbringing. But, of course, they are never going to be sitting together while he tells her about his classical morning torture. No more than he will get to tell her about how he sat the whole night by her garden fence one-and-a-half decades ago, downing a pint-sized bottle of cognac. She was aware of him that evening, though not aware he spent the whole night so close to her. And, of course, knew nothing of the way he hummed lines from a folk song he would never care to mention by name, even less to listen to again.

•

He can see all the better now the great formlessness of which that period of his life had consisted.

•

Sara had told him she really liked him. In a manner that made it impossible for him to interpret it as anything other than from the heart. And so he again asks himself what business she had had with a boy convicted of a crime. A boy who would have barged over to Sara with a cognac bottle and broken it over her head, if she had declined his visit (something G. himself had to put up with)—but that would have required the cognac bottle to have been in Aron's hands, not G's, in the first place. He has no interest, in fact, none at all, in recalling the incident, because nothing bores him more than contemplating violence and crime. Decidedly, especially when it concerns drugs. The album by the French countertenor Philippe Jaroussky, *Opium*, is perhaps the only drug-related thing in his life. Perhaps his pursuit of this man Aron Cesar from post office to bookshop could be categorized as some kind of crime. Because it flits into his mind that he should trail Aron a while. He has nothing to do right now. The only thing on his agenda this dreary, rainy day is to mail his assembled package. Surely that can wait a day; it has taken him several months already to get the thing together. Of course, he could have sent the thing by email, he still could, but computer mail suffers the same way as a person traveling by air rather than sea suffers: the mind does not move at the speed of the traveling body.

•

But does he really have nothing to do? No errands? Does this man, who now finds himself in the underworld, have something more to do than G. himself? Is Aron's undertaking more important than his? He recalls that the FIFA World Cup is going on. Because of this, so many people have so much to do these days. Their days are full, as the poem says. Even his father, an elderly man, almost fifty years older than G., follows this sport, soccer, withdrawing to the TV screen, though admittedly mainly when the German national team is on. And so that he can enjoy the game to the utmost, he goes over to see his nephew, who has in his living room a screen that covers an entire wall. G. has seen the screen himself, he once visited his cousin with his father, who had absolutely not exaggerated the size of the object, although perhaps the display only covered a half wall. His father's visits to his alcoholic nephew are, in G.'s mother's eyes, a source of joy, but also something to fear: for their duration, she knows where her husband is, in the literal sense, but she can also expect him to return home drunk. And because it has happened that his father returned home from his nephew's very drunk, that reminds G. of the last time the German national team played the English; doubtlessly the match was somewhat difficult for his father, since England is no less his favorite than Germany.

•

Their days are full.

•

As resolutely as he avoids keeping up with news about sports, in the media or from other people, not that he is ever around other people, he has become aware of a peculiar fact: due to their past achievements, some soccer teams are sure to win every time they play; the struggle of the opposing team selected to play against them is a mere formality, the way a bull in the ring never has a chance against the one hired to kill it. Even when the animal manages to drive its horns in. G. imagines a game of soccer with only one team playing in a stadium, still in front of a sold-out crowd. A bullfight without the bull. Sun without shadow.

•

My days have become full. That's the line in its correct form. But what's the poem from which the line comes? I promise myself I'll look it up when I get home later today, or whenever; I know which book the poem's in. It's a translation, a foreign poem. The book is one of two my parents' former tenant, who lived in the basement apartment where I now live, left behind when he moved out. When someone leaves something behind, someone else always comes to gather it up.

•

Someone else; me. Him, I mean. And he is thinking about his parents. But when he thinks about them, it's not that he's concerned about them, or that he is thinking of them generally, as one might imagine he should, this thirty-five-year-old man, given that they, his parents, are in their eighties. When he thinks of them, it's more like he sees a picture of them, what they look like and the way they sound when they open their mouths or stir themselves. He often imagines how they'll look when they're dead. Because their inevitable deaths are not so far off in the future. Close enough, even, that he's already pondering the possibility of using the whole house, wondering whether he'll leave Aragata, if it will give way to another address. When he was five or six years old, his mother took a photograph of him. They did not make a habit of taking pictures, she and his father. He reckons he could count on one hand the negatives they took to get developed when he was a child and teenager. But he was missing from the picture his mother took of him in the kitchen. He ended up just outside the frame. He remembers his father thinking this was funny, but he also remembers his mother not laughing. And when he recalls this incident, he realizes he has never seen his mother laugh. Not once. Such a thing would surely affect a child's development, regardless of whether his parents are fifty or twenty. And he realizes at once that *he* never laughs, either. He doesn't even smile. It didn't help that, as a child, he was made to listen to violin sonatas, piano trios, even entire concertos every morning over breakfast. He feels certain that the continuous stress the music of Delius and Schumann placed on the nerves of all of them had considerable impact on his mood and personality. He puts it thus, "all of them," because he knows his parents expressly used music to provoke one another, as well as him. They still do, though now they are offered fewer opportunities than before. But all the drama, all the tension in people's relationships, has to some degree a constructive effect. He himself is not a man of particular drama, but where drama is to be found, he's aware of it. For example, he is sure that his love for particular types of poetry, even his attitude in general toward his environment, is due to the delicate sections of the music that was forced upon him in his early childhood. Because precisely there, in those more delicate, sensitive parts, different strands appeared, thrashing among themselves for attention. It hardly needs mentioning that all this led him toward *la mélodie française*, the French version of the *lieder*, which is where he more or less exists in his mind from day to day. *Luxe, calme et volupté.* Everything he is not.

Luxurious, tranquil, and sensual. A person always seeks what he does not possess, of course. *Des meubles luisants, polis par les ans, décoreraient notre chamber* . . . Had these verses meant anything before Henri Duparc took them and set them to music? In fact, as soon as he thinks about these words, he wants to return immediately to Aragata, so that he can hear them sung. In his living room. What is he doing here in downtown Reykjavík when he could be at home, surrounded by his furniture, which is, after a fashion, meticulously polished by time, as in the poem? But he *is* in town, on a particular mission. He had intended to mail his envelope.

•

Aron comes back up from the basement. He looks about the place for a few moments, as if he is trying to make up his mind whether he has any reason to stay here longer, then walks toward the stairs up to the main part of the store. Perhaps G. still has his father and soccer on his mind, for when he looks at the half-Brazilian going up the stairs, he suspects Aron fastidiously keeps up with the World Cup. He's one of the busy. Right now, Aron's days are full. Unlike his own days. Or are they? G. knows there is a match in the tournament today because he saw it in the paper this morning. It is only now that it sinks in that the competition is being held in the homeland of Aron Cesar Óskarson's father. He watches Aron walk toward the magazines.

•

When he runs into a group of tourists in warm clothes on the stairs up to the main floor, a few lines from the poem about the redhead come to mind; they come to mind when he thinks about the red-haired Sara. *Here I am before all of you,* and so on. It looks like he is going to have to wait a while, because the tourists don't seem to see him standing below them on the steps. They have closed off the passageway for his journey, closed it completely. *Here I am before all of you, a man full of good sense, knowing life and death* . . . One of the tourists tugs at another, and they let him pass. Aron Cesar is standing flipping through a magazine. G. moves toward him. Planning to give himself more leeway, so that it will be possible to follow Aron beyond the shop, he decides to allow Aron to notice him and thus remove any doubt as to whether he recognizes him. G. stands beside Aron and reaches for a magazine right in front of his eyes. He feels like he's entering some kind of sports or pop culture world, because an impossibly powerful smell of perfume or aftershave rises off Aron, a smell which brings to G.'s mind the idea that some baseball superstar or an English boy band sells the product, have given their name to it. Before G. is able to compel Aron's attention, he notices the magazine Aron is paging through is *Haus und Garten*. He knows it well. His mother buys it sometimes, although it's never led to any changes to their home on Aragata. It is only down in his basement that the décor changes, down there with him where the magazines always end up. He clears his throat and stretches for *Interior Design*, a magazine of a similar type as *Haus und Garten*, and his plan takes material shape. Aron looks at him out the corner of his eyes, and G. can tell at once that

Aron doesn't recognize the person he is regarding: he has never seen him before. Not true. They have met in the street. They have even sat opposite one another on the bus, back in the years Aron and Sara were together, though Sara was not with him at the time.

•

If I were so inclined, I'd perhaps think it comical to see two young men standing side by side scrutinizing home and lifestyle magazines. And maybe Aron Cesar, at that moment literally choking me with his fragrance, thinks along similar lines, because at the edge of my vision I see him smile, and for a moment it occurs to me that despite everything he knows who I am, that someone has on some occasion pointed me out to him, smiling or laughing, saying that this was the guy who was making advances at Sara after Aron's relationship with her collapsed. This is the one who invited Sara to his house that time, but she didn't have time to stay, though she'd planned to, because her mother phoned shortly after she came inside, requiring that Sara drive her to Skálholt to play in a concert, because Sara's father had let her down.

•

Once again, music starts up from Aron's phone. Before he answers, he looks around, not entirely without a degree of nervousness, and briefly his eyes light on me. Once he starts talking, I take the magazine over to a display table about two feet from him.

I can still hear everything he says from that distance; it's soon clear he's making an appointment with his interlocutor. He mentions Þingholtsstræti. At first, it's like he does not recognize the street name, but once he has understood, he asks the person on the phone about the name on the door. I myself cannot hear the name; Aron keeps the information to himself. "What's that? Aren't we talking about five?" Five what? I ask myself. Five grams? "Very good," says Aron. "Very good. Very nice." Five grams of what? Is five grams a lot or a little of what's being discussed? After a short pause he says: "*Natürlich*. But what should it be? I know. *Haus und Garten*." Then he begins to explain. But the person he speaks to clearly knows what *Haus und Garten* means. He and Aron agree to meet in forty-five minutes, and the call ends.

•

Aron puts down the magazine, moves further to the left and chooses another magazine to look at. G. notices he picks from the music magazine shelf. He entertains the absurd idea that it's *Gramophone* or *BBC Music Magazine* that Aron has decided to look at, not the type of magazine he's used to browsing. G. starts to think of a certain piece of music, not a violin sonata this time, though, but a quartet by his favorite French composer, and consequently thinks about Sara, because her name sounds like the title of one of the composer's works for piano. He loves that work, no less than he does the quartet. How much fun it would have been to chat about that music with Sara. She really would have enjoyed talking about how badly her mother and her companions played the quartet. They certainly played it once, G. knows for sure, they played it in a concert at the National Gallery. They got a terrible review in the free paper that daily drops through G.'s mail slot. G. would have tried to defend the mother from Sara's attacks, which would only have caused Sara to heap more vitriol upon her. Would she have smiled or laughed over the terrible review her mother got? Would *he* have smiled, even?

•

"Of course, they were quite the fashionable couple." He imagines hearing a certain person, who happens to be his mother's close friend, say these words about the former couple. But wasn't that the way most people thought about the young couple at the time? He did not need any friend of his mother to point out the obvious truth. The obvious falsity. A friend who is, moreover, dead, he now remembers. She died on board a cruise ship, she had a stroke at sea, after being in the Caribbean. In G.'s eyes, Aron is the almost perfect opposite of beautiful or fashionable. His scent, which has not lessened even after G. has moved six feet away from him, is indeed a certification of the fact that he does not have very good taste. But alongside the red-haired Sara, Aron was an impressive, youthful, promising boy, in the eyes of so many, so dark and toned and . . . But is he still? Is that something he was ever? His physique, the way his buttocks lift at every step, how everything around him withers and dies as he goes about his business, all seems governed by pride, all built on a misunderstanding inside his head. He does not even keep his back straight, standing there at the rack. He has become stooped from bending so long over filthy dining tables, plying his illegal trade.

•

But what sort of people commit crimes? This question raises another in his mind. What had he himself been doing at Sara's house? And what happened to her mother's violin, the instrument that disappeared from her parents' house that evening thirteen years ago, and never turned up? Should he tell the truth about his role? Should it not wait a while? The suspicion quite definitely lurked inside at least one person, because Sara was well aware what happened to the violin, at least who it was who took it from the windowsill, she knew all too well, she had not wanted to know that he, G., was outside her house that night acting like a cat trying to attract mates, spraying piss on the walls of the house, in a most desperate state. Could it be that she had not told her mother of her suspicions because she disliked her that much? But why the enmity toward her? What had caused the tension between mother and daughter? Did it have something to do with Sara's relationship with Aron? No. But yes, too. He knows it did because Sara told him so herself, on one of the few occasions that they actually talked. It happened not when she came to his home, she was only there briefly, too briefly to have time to talk about her mother, though for sure she had cursed her about the drive to Skálholt. Their "real" chat happened on another occasion, so ordinary that he does not want to name it. The stiffness in her relationship with her mother was actually not unlike the roots causing frustrations between himself and his own parents. Music. Sara's mother had always imagined her daughter would take the violin out of her hands, or get her own, rather, so that they could play together, presumably her father's music, but Sara had never tolerated the dry, sawing sorrow of the violin, the sound the instrument produces in a beginner's grip. It occurs to him now, although he doesn't like the idea, that Sara had embarked on her relationship with Aron as some kind of rebellion against her mother.

•

Aron is back on the phone. This time the conversation doesn't concern commercial matters, like the earlier call. Now he's talking about something that happened yesterday, something that was a lot of fun. I have no intention of repeating the words he uses about the thing he felt counted as fun.

•

Does Aron know his father's language? He certainly has the appearance of a person from whom Portuguese should flow like a brook from mountain—but not all that glitters is gold, as my mother would say. From what I've heard so far from his mouth, nothing spills out but wretched Icelandic rocks mixed with the grit and dust of unseemly English loanwords.

•

When Aron drops the magazine on the floor and bends to pick it up again, G. sees what type of magazine it is. It isn't about classical music. "Did I tell you who I hit up yesterday?" Aron says, half whispering into the phone while he grabs the magazine and rolls it up, like he's trying to claim ownership of it. G. strains forward to hear who Aron met yesterday, but as he says the name into the phone two foreign men come past G. and their exotic language, something Slavic, distracts him from Aron. Since G. thinks he understands some of the words the men are saying, he is barely able to concentrate on what Aron adds next, but he manages to make out, however, that "she," presumably whomever he met yesterday, lives on Barónsstígur, "want to go there with me tonight?" He also hears Aron call his interlocutor "Eddi."

•

Eddi and Aron. Barónsstígur. G. returns *Interior Design*, and picks up a music magazine. And then he hears the name of the woman Aron was saying he met the day before. "Her name is Nóra. No, just Nóra. I think so, anyway. I only met her yesterday," he says. And he laughs. He reiterates to "Eddi" that "she definitely won't mind." But he doesn't hear any more; Aron lowers his voice. The Eastern Europeans on his other side occupy his attention further by saying something funny and laughing unnecessarily loudly.

•

Nóra? Is that an Icelandic name? To whom did the name Nóra belong? Rather than seeing before him some woman with this name, he imagines a black cat wearing it on a small tag hanging from the collar around its neck. Sara's hair was no less like a cat's.

•

She invited him. Not exactly to come visit, but she said that he should knock on her door if he was passing through the neighborhood. That was six months after her curtailed visit, likely nine or ten months after she and Aron were through. And he made up an errand in Seltjarnarnes, he pretended he had been to Grótta, the lighthouse at the end of the peninsula.

•

She lived in a tiny house in the garden of her parents' detached house, a building no doubt originally intended as a storage shed or some sort of outhouse. On the door was a sign that G. remembered a little tree branch had been hooked into, curving forward, as if at once to welcome a person and ward him off. It was a Friday evening. And he had been drinking. He does not anymore, it's important to say. And never really has, except for a few times in those peculiar years. But when Sara came to the door, she did not want to see him. He said he had been touring the lighthouse, but that did not sound convincing, at least not to her ears. But if she really had something else to do, as she told him while he stood there in front of the door, it was something she obviously made up on the spot. A lie, to put it plainly. And she paid for the lie. Or her mother did, rather. It was not in his character to use such expressions, "paying for," but the crime he committed that evening calls for crass language. There was no doubt Sara's parents, the composer and the violinist, were hosting some gathering. A low drone hummed from inside the house, so it must have been rather noisy inside, and after Sara sent him away, he noticed how intolerably the murmuring got on his nerves. Yet at the same time it drew him toward the house. Her mother must have been playing her instrument for her guests that evening, because otherwise she would have hardly left it on the windowsill in the living room. Aside from being a ridiculous place to set such a sensitive and precious possession as a violin, the windowsill was hot from the radiator turned on beneath it. The violin was warm to the touch as he reached into the open window for it. But why did he reach for it? What was going through his mind as he did so? He imagined the wood of the secretary he would one day own being as glossy as the instrument's wood. No, he didn't. Not at that moment. That happened later. He only knows he drank a pint bottle of brandy that night, and he knocked on the door of the girl he imagined he was in love with. Half the bottle was already in his bloodstream by the time he reached through the window, and so only half of his head was working, if that much. The second half of bottle went down inside him after he had stolen the violin, while he was sitting by her fence feeling sorry for himself. He does not even remember whether it was a cold or warm evening. Did he know at that moment the memory of the violin, the bottle and the fence paneling, and of the pitiful folk melody and lyrics resounding in his head, would be more important than some description of the weather in Seltjarnarnes? He knows only that he conducted himself in the way he would have expected the half-Brazilian Aron Cesar to, had the same situation lay before him. But what is Aron doing now? At this very moment? He slides the phone into his pocket and sets the magazine down, rolled up and no longer in saleable condition, on the table display by which I am standing. And he, Aron, determinedly strides out of the store.

•

I return my magazine to the rack where it belongs, not on the table like Aron, and follow him. It is still raining. I had actually read a little news in the music magazine that gave me considerable pleasure. Like a little sunbeam in all the gray moments, although I would never use such a simile myself. Aron heads directly across the street and into the supermarket on the right side of the post office. I am not going to mention the name of this store, no more than I mentioned the name of the folk singer earlier, or the magazine Aron was looking at. In truth, it's the supermarket a singer with a guitar often sits outside; I assume he wants compensation for his contribution to the noise pollution along the street. I have more than once heard him sing a song by the aforementioned folk singer. The one who wrote that ridiculous song. How did it go, again? *So easy to look at, so hard to define.*

•

Once G. is inside the supermarket, it pops into his mind that he could hurry the envelope over to the post office while Aron decides what to buy. He seems to be taking his time here. He is poking into this and that, just to have something to do. Aron has been forced to kill time until he is expected on Þingholtsstræti. But what should he himself do? Make haste to the adjacent building with the envelope? Is he entirely confident about the title he's chosen? Was it perhaps a blessing that Aron was unexpectedly there in the post office? Is hesitation in this case a victory? He does not entirely trust that he will be able to get to the post office and back; he realizes he does not want to lose Aron. As he watches him take a plum from the fruit table and roll it in his hand, thumbing its skin, a vivid picture of Aron comes to mind, inspired by the pages of the magazine he was looking at in the bookstore. He sees a hot climate, tropical, a pool, palm trees in the background; Aron is lightly-dressed, his proudly-displayed skin the color of milky coffee, enjoying life to the hilt, and he imagines how good Aron and Sara must have looked with so few clothes on. Together. And, following from this, getting naked. She with her light skin and rust-red, long hair. Again he hears, from his mother's friend's lips, that word: *fashionable.*

•

Aron decides to buy plums. G. slips over to the dairy cooler, then turns his back to Aron as the latter strides over to the milk products and plucks something G. thinks is yogurt. From there, Aron goes back past the fruit and vegetables, and fetches himself a croissant. G. trails after him as he goes to the cash register to pay. To maintain a distance between them, he lets one customer separate them in line. It just so happens that the man is double Aron's width, this is a man who ought to appear in a PSA about this kiosk wanting to falsely call itself a supermarket. G. hears Aron ask for a pack of cigarettes. "And a lighter, too," he adds. Once again G. is struck by how inconceivable it is that this Icelandic voice, as pubescent as it is in spite of emerging from a thirty-something-year-old man, should also know how to speak Portuguese. That Aron Cesar Óskarson is in his mid-thirties is no less absurd. When did he last see him? *My youth is dead like the spring*. It wasn't so long ago they were both as alive as a biting, crackling winter. As the fiery autumn that ignites winter. Only thirteen years have passed since Sara was getting hot between the sheets with Aron. And one year fewer since she received that letter from G. He has long wondered whether she read it under those very covers, and what she did with it after she'd read it. Had she thrust it into a desk drawer, a drawer she had thought would store letters from Aron, if Aron sent her any? All he knows is that the words of the letter followed her to where she later went. Which wasn't so much later. He knows it as well as . . . as well as what? As much as Aron Cesar is self-assured, his mind answers. As well as the fact that men like Aron send no letters. There are only notices. Not from him, but from the authorities, saying he has broken the law. That he is beyond repair. That he would be more at home in Brazil, in the City of God. *And a lighter, too*. I need to set light to something. Did Sara set light to his letter after reading it? He pictures a blue fire eating up the paper, while the flame from the candle is yellow. That Aron is still twenty. That inside him, a red fire burns. That he still dreams about lying under palm trees, his lighter next to the sun lounger, ready to set light to anything, to destroy anything casting a shadow over him.

Five Minutes Later

It is not without pangs of hunger that he observes Aron eating his store-bought snacks. It has stopped raining for a while, it seems, and Aron seems satisfied to sit on the stairs at Bernhöftstorfa. He spreads the plastic bag from the store on the stairs before he sits down. G. has to content himself with standing there contemplating Aron. He positions himself slightly further up, by a restaurant on Bankastræti, one named for the hill's slope: Banker's Hill. On the way here, Aron had stuck his nose briefly in the door of a small bar on Austurstræti, between the bookstore and the diner called Hressingarskáli, and shouted a few words to the employees; he could hear they took the form of a question. It was some kind of sports bar, with large TV screens on the walls; he must have been asking about the game later today. As Aron reached the corner of Austurstræti and Lækjargata, G. noticed he studied his reflection in the window of the souvenir shop, and he halted for a few moments before making sure he looked okay, in order to cross from one street to the next. G. allowed himself to do the same thing as he reached the corner window. But what was the difference between the two as they regarded their reflections? Aron is wearing a hooded, waist-length, nylon anorak, with a fur collar; G. has on his mustard yellow corduroy jacket. Aron is in black sneakers and dark gray jeans, which G. has to admit do not go badly with the dark blue jacket, and he assumes Aron has on a dark-blue T-shirt or shirt, just barely visible beneath the jacket. G. is wearing old, grayish brown wool pants, which could well be his father's, or even grandfather's, but were left behind by a deceased uncle. His mother thought he could use them. He also got to choose a couple of old pieces of furniture from the uncle's estate, beautiful items no one in the family cared for. His pants go really well with his dark brown suede shoes. He's wearing, too, the overcoat that was a Christmas present from his parents, and under the corduroy jacket he has on a light pink turtleneck.

•

Aron starts to eat. He begins with the plum. He discards what he doesn't eat on the sidewalk at the foot of the stairs. Then he stuffs the croissant into his mouth, washing it down with the yogurt drink. I could never imagine sitting down at a table with this man. From where G. stands he cannot hear whether the movements of Aron's jaw give off any noises as he chews the mixture of yogurt and bread, and he cannot tell, either, whether he eats with his mouth open, but he can well imagine the expression on Sara's face, back then, watching her boyfriend eating in front of her. It is difficult enough having to imagine what happens to the food after it enters the body; one should be spared having to hear the sounds of it entering. But it is not just the food that needs getting rid of. Aron lets the yogurt packaging go the way of the plum remnants. Then he takes his phone from his pocket and begins to play with it, or so it seems. He looks over his shoulder, as if making sure no one is monitoring what he's doing. And lights himself a cigarette.

•

That G. himself has a cell phone in his coat pocket is not exactly of his own volition. His mother wants to be able to get hold of him. She's an invalid. She does not trust his father will be reachable at times when he has popped out for a bit and she desperately needs some assistance, which happens not infrequently. He, her son, also sometimes rings her when he's not at home. Not often. Usually he's at home. While he observes Aron Cesar toying with his phone, he gets the idea to call him. Why not? He could play a trick on him. He could pretend to be someone else. Although he does not know much about the functionality of his handset, he knows for certain that his number does not appear on the screen of the device he is calling. He asked specifically for the feature that reveals that information be removed; he does not want people to know it's him calling them. Why not ring up

Aron? On Aron's screen, the caller would be listed as unknown. But what should he say? What could he say? Should he sound threatening? Isn't an anonymous call innately threatening, in this time when telephone users generally know who's calling before they start a conversation? He could pretend to be conducting business with Aron, but prefer not to give his name. At that very moment, Aron's phone rings.

•

He moves closer. Not only to better hear what's being said: he would like to smell the cigarette smoke. Experiencing that smell, he returns to his high school years, out on the sidewalk in front of the school, that awful establishment almost next door to where he is now, feeling like he is present within the very walls of the buildings as he listens to Aron on the phone. He speaks like a nineteen-year-old thinking of skipping his next class.

•

What terrible memories I have of school. And worse still, memories about going to school. Sitting at the breakfast table with his parents, listening to Mom's smacking noises, Dad's middle finger tapping ceaselessly on the table as he reads through the newspaper. The morning music ritual had become rarer at that time: they tended to put something on the player when they were in the midst of some kind of conflict, or irritable from the day before, and he remembers, like it happened yesterday, what they played the last day, what it was he had had to endure before he reached the long-awaited moment of moving into the basement and becoming his own man. Personally, I am a lover of chamber music, as it's called; I've probably mentioned that before, but when it lurks as background to other sounds that automatically stretch it and tug at its notes and pollute it, it is no better than that noise pollution I find so irritating: the rustling for popcorn in paper bags at the movie theater. Brahms's String Sextet No. 2 is downright intolerable when those you are listening with are occupied with feeding themselves toast and cucumbers, and when emanating from these same people is an almost palpable remorse that has been built up and calloused over several decades. My own man. As I became the day after Brahms had been especially selected to aggravate me. From that day, I was free from the torture in the kitchen each morning. For sure, it took me no little time to clean the basement apartment and make it mine, not least because my parents' tenant, thrown out so I could enter in, was hardly a clean freak. In fact, I would have needed to hire some assistance with the cleaning which lay before me. The tenant did not just leave dirt and dust, he somehow managed to forget two books on the hall table, the same table I later polished up, and which classifies in my mind today as one of my favorite things. The books were publications that were later of great benefit to me, although I did not realize it at first. For a long time, I was afraid that the tenant would come back when he found out that he had forgotten the books, but it has not yet happened, seventeen years later. And my parents are still alive. And I am, too. Which is not something to be taken for granted.

•

But how does Aron live, how does he organize his space? I won't rule out that he lives in accommodation financed by his parents, his father being just as prosperous as I imagine him to be, some fishing mogul in Brazil, and his mother no less well off, but potentially his funding comes from others' misfortunes, mostly young people, through the transactions he conducts. He lives in some kind of penthouse. And I don't have to wait long for my suspicions to be confirmed. "Come by my loft," he says into the phone, talking to someone of the opposite sex, I can tell. I do not know if that constitutes a pleasant surprise for me, exactly, but it is nevertheless surprising to hear Aron describe his living situation to the girl on the phone. He takes considerable time in doing so, since he is clearly trying to entice the girl to come over. What I do not know at first, however, is that Aron is asking whether "she" can't come by some time tomorrow, maybe in the afternoon, the invitation somehow not fitting with how he recently asked a friend whether he wouldn't come with him this evening to some woman's place, a woman whom he said he met yesterday. But then I come to my senses. This is some totally different woman he wants to meet tomorrow. "Why don't you come up and see me around two tomorrow?" he asks. And I can tell from listening to him he gets an affirmative answer to the suggestion. "I'm actually busy today," he says. "Tonight? No, I need to meet a guy tonight." He's lying. Unless he was lying to his friend, although I still don't understand why he was inviting him on a date with the woman he met yesterday. Something has clearly gone over my head. Aron says goodbye to the woman on the phone and lights a second cigarette.

•

While he watches Aron smoke the cigarette, three men of a similar age as him come by, maybe a little older, walking along the sidewalk toward Bankastræti. They're bankers. The people who make decisions, G. thinks. Filled with fragile self-confidence, greedy for ever-higher wages. But all the signs indicate their wives or girlfriends chose their clothes for them, especially their shoes. Two of them are in black, short overcoats. The third is wearing a tight-fitting jacket and light blue shirt that stretches out past the jacket's cuffs. Why such narrow-toed shoes? They remind him of his mother's clock, its hands. He looks at his watch; it shows exactly twenty minutes past twelve. The midday news is about to begin on the National Radio. His father is preparing to turn on the radio, lunch in front of him on the table. Aron Cesar, on the other hand, is done eating, and the men from the bank are on their way to get sustenance. They walk past him, and he hears them talking about enjoying some dish, which they mention by name, how they could imagine getting such a thing again. They haven't *already* eaten, have they? No, they are on their way to get food. They walk down the steps to the sidewalk by the outdoor chess set, then down Lækjargata, and disappear inside the doors of the fast food restaurant next to the champagne bar, a place G. has always pictured as the scene of a crime, a crime with a capital C, one just now committed, still being committed, about to get committed. But what about himself? He realizes that maybe he should get something to eat. But this unexpected event on his agenda at the moment allows no such thing. By now Aron Cesar has risen to his feet, put on his hat, since it has started raining again, is brushing off his pants and preparing to walk off along the sidewalk, in the direction of Bankastræti. Without Aron noticing him, G. takes a few steps toward the high school. He feels sure Aron will head up Bankastræti, and does not therefore need to go after him immediately.

•

He pauses by the wall of the building that houses the Art Festival. And as he looks across Lækjargata, keeping an eye on Bankastræti, he sees the trio from the bank come back out the door of the fast food restaurant. One of them, the one dressed in the jacket, seems to be adjusting his coat, which indicates he'd taken it off, although they could not have been inside the place more than half a minute or so. He surmises from the men's gestures that the restaurant was not up to scratch, that they are trying to shake off its effect on them. Then one of them points to another nearby place, and they appear to almost at once decide to go in. But at that moment Aron has reached the sidewalk on Bankastræti. Time to go after him. The rain is worsening. G. imagines the three bankers anxious to take shelter, even more than to satisfy their hunger. Aron has reached the corner of Skólastræti by the time G. gets to Bankastræti. He is standing by the window of the store that used to be Hans Petersen, the camera store. Does Aron have any children? G. asks himself. Will they be waiting at home with their hungry beaks come the end of the workday? It may be he's fathered children—it's actually very likely—but they are not part of his life in the loft. What's more, he isn't returning home after the workday. His working day includes a visit to a woman he met the day before. And the next day: another visit from some other woman, coming to see him at his loft. Is he still caught up in the same thing as before, because everything else in his life, the things meant to be edifying or uplifting, have run aground in the sand and come to no good? Surely his parents' educations, the fact that they have their respective homes on separate continents, put pressure on him to learn a trade or science? What kind of job includes walking around town, a meeting in a house on Þingholtsstræti in the middle of the day, and still being able to afford a trip to a bar to watch soccer in the afternoon, which I know, which I think I know, is on Aron's agenda?

•

Þingholtsstræti is the next street over from Ingólfsstræti. I myself once had a job on that street, the job that is for all intents and purposes the only real job I've had in my entire life, with the exception of my so-called youth work experience. A medium employed me as a transcriber. It wasn't, of course, a full-time job. There would have needed to be more rapid contact between the worlds involved. But I remember seeing it as a real job at the time, I even thought quite highly of it. I felt like I had responsibilities, not least when I was sent to the corner of Þingholtsstræti and Bankastræti with film the medium needed developing. What added to this sensation that I was being entrusted with something important was the fact that my parents had never tried to instill any sense of trust in me. I would take the film to Hans Petersen, the photo shop. Actually, I think those rolls of film, which I am coming to realize were far, far greater in number than the scant few my parents treated our family to when I was a kid, must have contained very few, if any, actual pictures of the séances. Kristján, the guy who organized them, and the guy who finally fired me, used to take pictures of the participants before meetings began. Truly peculiar photographs. There would usually be seven to eight people, typically a mix of genders, and he arranged the group a bit like a soccer team along the wall of the room where I was situated at my desk, seeming to make a big deal about the fact that people shouldn't smile or have unnecessarily joyful expressions. Yet I think it quite probable that one of the many rolls I took to get developed had been shot during a séance. "There's nothing on this film," the woman who served me said, "It's blank." Just like Mom's image of me in the kitchen. Although the kitchen was visible. I remember the woman at Hans Petersen asked me if I was working for Kristján on the corner, as she put it, and although she had this slightly odd expression, or perhaps *because* she did, I didn't think it made my job less meaningful to have been asked this. Not until several days later, that is, when I remembered the question in the wake of having seen Kristján at an embarrassing moment; namely, I barged in on him in the middle of a certain private ceremony, one I feel rather uncomfortable mentioning by name. He had not expected me to be in his house at that time of the day, before noon, because I tended to turn up in the afternoon and stay until evening, often until the séance itself. This unpleasant insight into his life led, several days later, to him firing me. People don't want to have in front of their eyes those who remind them of how inappropriate their private acts become in front of others. Now, at this very moment, Aron is turning onto the street to which his errand summons him.

•

When he's gone roughly ten feet along Þingholtsstræti, he suddenly turns around, like he's left something behind. I lean toward the window of the clothing store on the corner and pretend to be busy with something other than following him: I open my bag and appear occupied getting something out of it. I take out the envelope with the manuscript, and feel for a moment like the one hundred and fifty-one manuscript pages are closer to three hundred. Then I turn back to see Aron standing in front of the steps to Caruso, examining the printed menu in the frame on the stair railing. Didn't he just finish eating? The weather has cleared up for now, but more precipitation looks likely. It's plausible that the improving weather's effect on Aron Cesar is to make him want something refreshing to drink. He wants a beer. But does he drink? If you're partaking of the green herb, would you also drink? I recall the news story about the poet who killed someone inside this very restaurant eight or nine years back. I will never forget the man's name, although I don't know what he wrote. But I wonder what's it's like to be a poet with a poetic name: Svanur, the name of that poetic bird, the swan? Not good, I imagine. But perhaps it benefits a poet to kill someone? G. remembers an Icelandic literary critic once complaining that domestic authors generally did not have the requisite life hazards to have anything remarkable to say in their poetry. Would homicide be considered a hazard for the one committing it? According to what G. read in the news about the killing at Caruso, the poet was not in danger from the photographer at the moment he killed him. It came to light later that the poet had had dealings with the photographer, involving the latter taking a picture of him at some unfortunate moment in the poet's life, an image published in a prominent place in a major newspaper. And instead of writing about the experience, the poet killed his subject. G. sees Aron place his finger on a particular dish on the menu, and move closer to see better. Then he goes off along the sidewalk, and soon crosses the street, toward the house where the séances took place. His step is lighter than earlier; perhaps he's looking forward to seeing someone. G. knows he is allowing himself to look forward to something.

•

As he starts to walk in the same direction as Aron, he happens to glance up at the house where he worked, and cannot understand how it can be that this is the first time he's found it strange that the séances took place in such a busy, noisy area as this part of downtown. And, simultaneously, he remembers having read in the paper or heard on the radio, though he seldom engages with media, that this particular corner in downtown Reykjavík is the most dangerous street corner in the whole of Europe at certain times of day or night—presumably on weekend nights.

•

Even though it's barely ten years ago that he received his unexpected insight into the world of spiritualists, he now feels like it's unthinkable that there's any life left in that world today. But as he thinks along these lines, he wonders if he sees the present as so modern that ten years in the past becomes more or less ancient history. A decade-and-a-half back, the twenty-something Aron Cesar was caught up in drugs. It does not look like anything has changed. Has that world, the world of drugs, not moved on, become outdated, in the same way he imagines the spiritualist world has? Are the substances that Aron is taking to a man on Þingholtsstræti perhaps totally different, more modern, than the ones Aron himself used back when he was twenty or so? *I know as much as any one man can know about the ancient and the modern . . .* One need not delve very deep into the nature of these two aspects of culture, drugs and the supernatural, to see that they have at least one thing in common: Hallucinations. Although sometimes G. had loved to transcribe the conversations that took place in the séance—especially when the medium needed to arrange his flow of information from the other side in accordance with, or rather not in accordance with, information the participants were not ready to accept as being correct—he is probably as little excited by the world of spiritualism as he is

by the world of forbidden substances being sold in secret. The
sort Aron Cesar is about to take into this house here in the city
center. *Haus und Garten.* Will he get to hear him say those words
into the intercom? No. It does not happen. Aron goes into a passageway, and disappears from his sight. The doors are obviously
around back.

•

I had no idea until now that the square where I was sitting down
to wait for Aron was called Bríetartorg: Bríet's Square. It's on
the corner of Amtmannsstígur and Þingholtsstræti, and it's really
hardly a square, more like a corner lot on which no house has
been built. Possibly there was a house here once, but no longer;
it's vacant. I think I mentioned it before, but maybe not, that I
tend to have trouble deciding what I feel about my own feelings,
or, rather, trouble assessing whether what I feel is really what I
feel, whether it is in general not simply what I think I should
feel. And once again I come up against this question as I consider
whether I ought to be proud that I know who this Bríet was.
And therefore know what she did to merit having a little square
named after her. Aron wouldn't know that. But how long is he
planning to be inside?

•

While G. speculates that she must be about to call him, his
mother, he decides to follow up on his idea of calling Aron Cesar,

as he earlier conceived. It is time to play his prank. He gets up and walks a few steps toward the house Aron went into. It is diagonally right, opposite the square. He scans for movement in the windows of the house, but at first glance sees nothing, even though none of the blinds are down. The basement windows are slightly buried, and the bottom parts of the first-floor windows are approximately a person's height from the sidewalk. The house is obviously newly renovated. It's like he remembers this house had seemed in rather bad shape when he last saw it. The white window frames give the appearance of confidence, and the unpainted corrugated iron is a sign that the siding panels were set very recently. They always leave corrugated iron unpainted for the first year. But why? Why does he know this about corrugation? He has never held a paintbrush, or driven nails into a wall, not even one time in his high school work experience program. In all likelihood, it's totally idiotic to be calling Aron. But if he rings him, should he then immediately say a name? It is ridiculous to be calling him. But it's also ridiculous to wait here outside this house and not call him, given that he's had the idea in the first place. He sits back down on the bench. Would he not in truth be doing Aron a favor by causing him to take the phone out of his pocket in front of the man in the apartment? Would it not indicate how sought after business with him is? He gets the phone out of his pocket, and it takes him a short time to get Aron's number from directory services. "Do you want me to connect you directly?" The girl who gives him the number offers to do that, or something like it. But he declines. As he types in the number, two teachers walk past whom he knows from high school, they are on the Amtmannsstígur side, on the side nearer him. He does nothing to reduce the chances of them seeing him; they would not recognize him, even though one of them taught him one winter in school. The call gets answered. He waits. "Hello?" He waits a little longer. "Is that Aron Óskarson?" he asks, when Aron seems like he's not going to say anything else. "Who's speaking?" asks Aron. "Is this Aron Cesar?" asks G. "It depends on who's asking," says Aron. G. allows a few beats to pass. "Who is this?" asks Aron again. "Do you have anything for me?" G. says in reply, and feels the way his heart beats faster. "What do you mean?" asks Aron. "Who is this speaking?" Yes, who is this? G. asks himself. Who do I imagine this is? "I'm asking if you have some stuff for me," he says, placing his left hand on his chest, as if to slow the beating. "Some what?" asks Aron. "You know what I mean," says G. "No, I don't," says Aron. Does he detect impatience in Aron's voice? G. tries to imagine a glimpse of the face Aron will be making to the man living in the apartment. "I'm asking if you have anything. I need it today." To those words, Aron responds with something approaching aggressiveness. "What the hell are you talking about?" he shouts. "Who gave you my number?" Without realizing it, he has let the cat out of the bag. *Who gave you my number?* G. decides to play another prank, and marvels at his own daring—at first glance, to an external observer, as he puts it himself, daring is not the foremost character trait one would associate with him. How many thoughts fit into the very short time period between a question and its response? "Nóra," says G. The idea arrives completely from the blue. And Aron repeats her name. "*Nóra?* Who are you?" he asks. "It doesn't matter," replies G. "I'm just looking for some stuff, and I was told to call you. By Nóra." "You're messing around with me," says Aron, asking again who this is. There is despair in his voice, mixed with nervous laughter. "I'll just have to look somewhere else," G. pulls out this suitable answer, but before he disconnects, he clears his throat. The throat-clearing is the last thing Aron will hear over the phone. It is starting to rain again. G. hadn't meant to clear his throat, but in retrospect he is fairly certain he has done the right thing. Possibly he'd seen this done in such situations in a movie, one time, the character in the movie having rung up someone without giving his name, and then clearing his throat when he felt enough had been said, as a way to end the call.

•

He shouldn't have done this. Involuntarily, he stands up from the bench and heads the other way, where the two teachers went, up toward Ingólfsstræti. No, why should he *not* have done this? The rain intensifies. If anyone is surveilling him, he will undoubtedly attract more suspicion by looking away from the building rather than toward it. He turns back again, and goes directly across the street; he heads along the sidewalk toward Bankastræti, past the building where Aron is inside. And, needless to say, he is talking with the man: as he passes the first window on the first floor, none other than Aron Cesar is on the other side of the glass. He is looking out, and from the perspective G. has, from under Aron's neck, he strikes G. as rather pale in his appearance. But that must be his imagination. He is not going to let himself off the hook, pretend he is not somewhat imagining, that he is not under the influence of the way things are in movies. And without being tempted to look in Aron's direction in the window, although perhaps he does squint his eyes just slightly toward him, he can be totally confident that, as far as Aron is concerned, G. is simply some passerby on his way along the street. Which he is. So Aron is to be found on the building's first floor. Now G. knows that.

•

Aron. Barónsstígur. Nóra? Why is that woman's name so familiar? Could it be that it came from the other side, from his time as a séance transcriber? How pale Aron was when he looked through the window! Had the color in his face, the lack of it, been a figment of the imagination? But of course—G. had managed to strike terror in Aron's heart with the mention of Nóra's name. The black cat awaiting its prey on Barónsstígur.

•

It's probably been ten minutes since Aron stood in the same spot G. stands now: at the door to Caruso, in front of the framed menu. G. allows himself to think that the menu is the same as when the poet killed the photographer nearly ten years back. It was in the lavatory inside this building that the atrocity had taken place. But had they finished ordering? Was their order on the way to their table at the time Svanur shoved the photographer against the sink? G. had not intended to stand so long at the door to Caruso. For the rain is intensifying, the drops ceasing to be drops, turning instead into long rods condensed together as if *it's raining women's voices as if they are dead even in memory*, to quote another poem by the author of "The Redhead," the poem about rain. *The old and the new.*

•

The next moment, the two come face to face, the old and new, everything coming together out in the rain. The phone rings, and G. reckons he knows at once who is calling him. Right up until the next moment, when he sees Aron coming out of the passageway back onto the street. Aron is holding an open umbrella, which he must have borrowed from the man he met, or been given it as a thanks for his welcome business; with his free hand he presses his cell phone to his ear. It occurs to G. that the number-concealing powers of his phone must have failed, that Aron is calling him, wanting to ask who was interrupting him earlier with indecipherable requests. No, he is talking to Nóra. He must be talking to Nóra. For it is not Aron's voice that G. hears when his phone establishes its connection; it is his mother's voice. "Hi, Mom." He's made it to shelter under a kind of awning protruding from the wall above the door to another restaurant on the street, approximately thirty feet from Caruso. "Where are you?" It actually suits him rather well that his mother should call just as Aron comes back out into the open air, because he thinks that, as he huddles under the shelter, a phone call to his mother makes him invisible to Aron, now strolling along the street toward him. He tells her that he is in town. "What are you doing in town?" she asks. "I had an errand," he says. He cannot see whether Aron pays any attention from where he stands under the shelter, even though he almost brushes past him as he walks by. "I don't know where your father is, either," says his mother. *Either?* G. thinks to himself. She scolds him, her son, because she does not know where his father, her husband, is. "He was headed out for rolls and salami this morning, but hasn't come back yet," she says, and continues with her story while G. hurries after Aron, who is at the corner of Bankastræti. "He'll turn up," G. says, and asks, as he watches Aron walk toward the next corner, at Ingólfsstræti: "Do you know who Ósk Völundardóttir is?" "Of course I know," replies his mother. "Wasn't she in Parliament?" he asks. "If you are talking about Ósk Völundardóttur Bjarnason, then yes, she was in Parliament," his mother says. "She lived in Brazil," he says. "She fled to the country, yes," she says. "But she's no longer in Parliament, right?" he asks. "No." His mother uses his name, but he does not care to repeat it here, he has never been fully satisfied with his own name. "But what are you doing in town?" she asks. "I was on the way to the post office," he says. "Oh, then I would've had you take these letters I need to send, you should've let me know. Why don't you tell me when you're going out like this?" He starts chasing Aron up Bankastræti. "I need to go back anyway," he says, and that somewhat heartens his mother. And she asks: "Today?" "I can go tomorrow," he says. "But are you there now?" she asks. "Isn't it pouring?" It's raining women's voices, he thinks to answer, and he even hears his mother gasp with surprise, as though she actually heard him recite the poet's verse. But instead he asks: "Doesn't she have a kid, Ósk?" "Why are you thinking about her?" His mother is noticeably surprised. "Do you usually think about the people in Parliament?" "No, I just saw her earlier here in town," he says. "Then she must be on a city break," she says. "Doesn't she have a kid?" he asks. "Did she have any kids with her?" his mother asks in response. "No," he answers, but as he's about to remind her of Ósk Völundardóttur's son, she takes the words from him. "She lives far in the north. She's a mayor somewhere, I can't remember whether in Húsavík or Dalvík." Aron has reached the corner of Skólavörðustígur and Bankastræti. He has a sprightlier step than before, despite the rain, and G. lets himself think that perhaps Aron is on some of what he sold the man on Þingholtsstræti. G. doesn't pretend to understand those sorts of transactions, he has no desire to have any such sense, but isn't it normal for a vendor to test the product himself in front of a buyer if a transaction is to be carried out, to convince the latter that the product is genuine? In order to bring his father back up as a topic of discussion, his mother tells him how his dad once chose this party, Ósk's, in the election, something she could never bring herself to do. The actual reason for her calling him, except for letting him know that his father has not returned home, is to ask him to get something for her from a pharmacy. And with a promise to do it for her, G. manages to shake the call. It is quite a different story, however, to shake off the wetness. The need for an umbrella is almost an emergency. He could get an umbrella by dashing briefly into the pharmacy a couple corners down, and take out two birds with one stone, but it is doubtful that he will be able to keep up with Aron after such a digression. Then Aron himself comes to his aid. He suddenly changes course across the road, and from his determined gait it's evident that he has some particular errand in the shop they both now head into. A shop G. knows is of Danish origin, without caring to mention its name. He knows umbrellas are sold there.

•

Aron heads straight for a display in the shop; he knows exactly what he is after. G. himself does not hesitate; he walks right up to the counter and says he wants one of the umbrellas hanging on racks that extend from the wall behind the boy at the check-out. It takes Aron a while to select what he wants to buy, long enough for G. to finish his transaction and take up position on the other side of the store, where he waits for Aron to head back out. In the meantime, he eyes some sunglasses, which he likes, not least because of how cheap they are. And he sneaks glances at the kid who served him, who is currently attending to Aron. He is an unusually handsome fellow, someone G. imagines could easily have an appearance not unlike Aron Cesar, if he wanted to. But this boy's make is different. G. sees before him one of the members of the French Ébène Quartet. Could he imagine himself serving in such a shop? How would he conduct himself if he was at this very moment selling Aron the notebook he had chosen? He would perhaps interject a little comment about the book, even praise Aron for his choice, but in such a way that Aron felt uncomfortable accepting it.

•

He notices that the boy at the checkout is looking at Aron, contemplating him, thinking something. He is thinking the same thing as G. himself.

•

It is the second violinist of the Quartet he has in mind, he remembers. The black-haired one.

•

He really should buy some sunglasses. Too late now, because Aron has turned away from the counter and is hastening toward the door. So they come out onto the street, both with raised umbrellas. Aron proceeds noticeably more slowly now, as though buying the notebook has calmed him.

•

One of the first people G. passes as they walk up Laugavegur is a young man he saw not long ago in the old cemetery, where he goes sometimes, especially in summer. A man who at first glance seemed to be a woman. He has long flowing hair, which is now hidden under a rain hat made of gleaming black plastic; he's wearing smooth, dark-purple corduroy pants, and a very narrow, light-brown suede jacket, double-breasted. What G. fixed in his memory when he saw him in the cemetery was how he crossed himself when they passed one another; what he especially notices this time is how he narrows his eyes at Aron, but then seems not to really notice G. as they pass each other in the very next moment. When he turns around to study this feminine figure a little longer, what crosses his mind is how the figure's gait is practiced, that he needs to remind himself at every step that he is a woman when he walks. But why did he cross himself when he saw me in the cemetery? And why did he not just now? If I were him, I would hurry to cover; it can't be at all good for his suede in drenching rain like this. Aron, however, has decided on his next stop. He pauses for a moment at a record-store window, framed by stone painted bright green, then heads across the street into a bar, one or two buildings farther up the street, a bar I know has a rather questionable reputation. Questionable reputation? How do I know that, I who never go into town? I'm making it up. As soon as Aron Cesar chooses a place the reputation of said place becomes questionable.

•

At a glance, G. cannot see that anything other than drinks are served at this establishment. He expects Aron is looking for a drink. Before he followed him into the bar, he waited a short

while outside, and when he entered, into air thick with a history
of cigarette smoke; Aron was standing at the bar, and the bartender was in the middle of serving him a beer. But of course G.
knows people are not allowed to smoke inside restaurants nowa-
days. This thick air is the dark face of this place, heavy with the
thoughts customers leave behind, for thought cannot be cleansed
away. He reaches for a magazine lying in the windowsill by the
entrance and sits down at a table next to the window, which
looks out onto the street. Aron seats himself on a high bar stool,
and G. hears him groan heavily as he sits. The bartender brings
him the drink, a tall glass full of golden, sparkling beer. He gets
the sense that Aron is a regular here, that he is at ease with himself here. He and the bartender don't talk to one another, but
he imagines that in Aron's world people usually don't converse,
except perhaps via phone, only when they want something. Aron
lifts the glass to his lips, takes a gulp, and sets it back on the
table. G. starts to think about counting the minutes until Aron's
phone rings. It must happen sooner rather than later. Someone
will need to reach him. He also thinks he knows that Aron is
preoccupied by the abrupt phone conversation earlier, debating
with himself whether he should believe Nóra, the woman he
has only just met, when she denied telling someone something.
As G. contemplates him sitting at the end of the bar, suddenly
he can't figure out why he is keeping up his pursuit. Did Aron
deserve this? If Aron realized someone was after him, would he
feel anything about it? That some individual, totally unrelated
to him, is sacrificing his time to pursue him? Does a man like

Aron understand anything other than what can be economi-
cally assessed? Would he understand the meaning of G. delaying
sending this story by mail, in order simply to be able to tail him?

•

Something tells him that his father will be much longer on his
bakery trip than the time required to buy rolls and salami. And
suddenly he is filled with the desire to have him sitting here, so
that they could get coffee together, father and son. Or a beer. His
father beer, him coffee. He would point out Aron to his father,
as Aron sits at the bar, and tell him that this is the man G. once
wished did not exist. "Like you yourself have sometimes wanted
Mom not to exist," he would add. And as soon as he imagines
the words, he realizes they, father and son, have never spoken
together like that before, that they have never really spoken
about what they wanted in life, or did not want. His father had
once asked if he could pass him a magazine lying on a foot stool
in their living room on Aragata, and he, G., had sometime later
turned down his father's invitation to come with him to a lec-
ture at the university, but they had never particularly expressed
themselves to each other, beyond that, not about their own matters, as G. mentally phrased it. And he adds a few words more to
what he imagines he would say to his father: "And like you have
perhaps wished about me, too, that I didn't exist." And his father
would reply: "Remember our trip to the Roman Baths. They
weren't, of course, Roman Baths, but a sort of spa, which neither
of us cared about, me or your mother. But you stayed back at the

hotel, while your mother and I went to rinse ourselves clean. And I felt like I had cleansed myself, not only of your mother, but of you, too. Or so I felt. You are correct, perhaps I have at some point wished you did not exist. Maybe I've thought something along those lines. But when we walked out of the bathhouse, your mother and I, I had no illusions that I was alone, I knew she was by my side when we walked out. And we went together to the hotel. And there you were. What I had wished had not come to pass." Then his father would gently pat his shoulder in a fatherly way, and say to him: "Don't forget to buy that cream for your mother." Then they would take a sip of coffee, or of beer, and be silent together a little while. But can G. remember what it's called, the thing he has to buy for his mother? Yes. The name of the cream indicates, to his ears, that many young women use such creams. Not Sara. She would not have used a perfume bearing this name, a name he translates faithfully over into Icelandic: *Viðgerð*. There are other women who need *viðgerð*. Sara is beyond that. Beyond *repair*, to use the English name. *Viðgerð*.

•

He decides to use the time while Aron is drinking his beer to run back to the pharmacy. Aron undoubtedly will sit for at least a quarter of an hour, if not half-an-hour, or more. Ten minutes would suffice for G. to go to the pharmacy, even if he pops into the Danish store en route and gets the sunglasses, as he is thinking of doing. When do bars like this open? And what time is it? It is not yet one. There is no one in here except G., Aron, and the bartender. And, actually, a middle-aged man in gray coveralls, in whose direction Aron looked when G. opened the door. It was like Aron thought the one in the coveralls had been the one who came in, not G., when the door opened. Which is odd. By right, Aron should have looked toward the door. But instead he looked toward the man in the coveralls.

•

It has cleared up when G. comes back out into the fresh air. I can see the way he squints his eyes when he opens the door, like the sun is shining. But the sun does not shine, although it is not raining, either.

Fifteen Minutes Later

For the second time today, he is on the way to the same bar. But this time his bag also contains sunglasses and skin cream. Should he put on the glasses before entering? *You whose mouth is made in the image of God. / A mouth which is Order itself.* At the drugstore counter, mouthwash was on sale, and he'd had great difficulty stopping himself from buying some. It occurs to him he could wait outside the bar for Aron to come out. The air inside was hardly palatable, and his return might raise suspicions, though no one except the man in coveralls seemed to have noticed him the first time. But when he re-enters the place, there's no Aron at the bar, just an empty beer glass. There's now some music on the loudspeaker system, and the music reminds him of the call

Aron got on his cell while inside the post office. The man in gray coveralls is still here; he has moved to the inner room, has only gone deeper in, and the way he holds his head and slumps over the table indicates that he does not feel too well. G. cannot see the bartender, but when he goes to the bar, and a thousand króna banknote has been left next to the empty beer glass, he curses himself for having gone to the pharmacy and lost Aron. At that moment the bartender reappears, and G. nods his head to him. "Did he leave, the guy who was here earlier?" he asks. "Aron? He's turning beer into water," says the bartender, and points to the empty glass. "He must have gone to the restroom." Then he asks if he can get G. anything, but G. wants nothing. He must get out. He has made a mistake.

•

It has started to rain again as he comes back out onto the sidewalk. He unfurls the umbrella and crosses Laugavegur, and it just so happens that he sees the man in the light-brown suede jacket, the one he saw cross himself in the cemetery. He's headed up Laugavegur. His jacket is darker than before, and there is a certain darkness over his whole person, in part because he's now carrying an umbrella. What G. suspected when he saw him earlier is confirmed now, that this man's gait loses its evident femininity if he cannot fully concentrate. The umbrella is distracting him. G. stations himself by the corner of the next building, the record shop, the one whose window Aron had looked into, and he watches the kid in suede disappear into the rain, amid the other pedestrians. G. likes standing in the rain, likes the sound of the drops when they patter against the taut nylon of his umbrella.

•

The street can thank the foreign tourists for how lively it is right now. And for a moment, G. reflects on how Aron Cesar should be grateful that he is following him, because he believes that Aron is somehow sad, and G. suspects there is something hanging over him that he wants to break free of. Although Aron evidently does not seem to lack people to chat to, G.'s image of him, alone at the bar, and of the empty glass he left on the table, is colored with tones that evoke sadness and compassion. This is a lonely man surrounded by people, he thinks. When Aron comes out of the bar, he is holding a shot glass, and has a cigarette in his mouth. He opens his umbrella, lights the cigarette and takes a drink. As he smokes he looks along the street, then toward the record store, looking so fixedly in this direction that G. begins to suspect he's planning to head there. Something in the window from earlier has attracted Aron's interest. He kills the cigarette, returns inside with the glass, and when he comes out again, goes straight across the street and into the store.

•

Had the bartender told Aron he'd been asked about while in the restroom? Could it be that Aron had failed to notice G. while he was in the bar? He can scarcely imagine that, although clearly Aron's eyes were focused on the man in the coveralls as G. opened the door. The two plus two that Aron is required to put together to get to four does not involve large numbers. Either he's pretending he has not noticed G., or G. has only been found out in his own imagination. How well does blocking your number work? He does not trust telecommunication any more than the communications he once served in his job as transcriber-assistant.

•

He allows a minute or two to pass before he follows. He has been in this store before. He once bought a Christmas gift for his parents here, a box set of piano music. Not just any music. However, he doesn't really want to think about it, because his parents had felt nothing over the gift. And the possibility that it could be returned, exchanged for something else instead, was never mentioned. His father and mother did not think in that way, exchanging things. He had simply not chosen the right music. And so he was met with silence.

•

Aron is on the upper floor of the store, a kind of mezzanine, not unlike the one in the bookstore on Austurstræti. He is looking at movies in plastic covers. There is a strong smell of incense. Not an aroma—an aroma is not this strong. G. regards the man at the register, trying to ascertain whether he was the one who lit the incense. Some slow, viscous rock music is playing. He knows what this is, this is Icelandic music. He nods to the guy at the counter, goes up to the mezzanine, and installs himself at the classical music rack. It was here he found the gift for his parents. Then Aron's phone rings and he sets down the movie he had been checking out before he answers the phone. G. cannot hear what Aron says very well because soon after he starts talking the music coming through the speakers begins to crescendo, and the time it takes to achieve its peak is about the length of Aron's call, roughly three to four minutes. All that time, Aron stands by the movie shelves, turning a few times toward the front of the store as if to make sure no one is eavesdropping. And what G. gathers from his conversation, roughly, is that Aron is tired of someone's incessant treachery, but he is planning to catch the game later, he is going to watch it on Austurstræti. Then he says to his conversation partner that he'll "take a cab to your place later." The last thing G. hears, just before the sensations of the music's peak drown out his words entirely, is whether he, the person with whom Aron is talking, remembers "The Dandy," the kid they always called "The Dandy." G. hears nothing more over the music. He buries himself right down in the CDs as Aron turns around to go down to the lower floor. And so that he seems immersed in his own world, G. flips through the "S" section of classical music; he has reached Schumann by the time there's no longer a risk Aron will identify him.

•

The Dandy? Did he make up the phrase or does it really exist? Is he himself inventing that word, or did it simply invent itself? He imagines that, every time he puts the CD in the music player, the one he gave his parents and now owns, having moved it from their collection on the upper floor down to his collection in the basement, his mother and father's silence increases beyond its usual level, that it somehow becomes louder and thicker, more material, if you can say that about silence. They have called down a curse upon themselves with their indifference to the gift he gave them. Have they ever used the word *dandy* about their son's tastes? Is Aron Cesar the first to do so? Have his parents ever called him "their boy"? Not that he remembers. It would be possible to count on one hand the times they have come down to the basement to see him since he moved there.

•

It doesn't seem that Aron is looking for anything particular in the store. He puts away his phone, flips through an arbitrarily chosen rack in the middle of the floor; when he goes over to the counter and addresses the employee, G. moves closer to the opening between the upper and lower floors in order to hear when Aron starts talking to him. "That smells terrible," he says, indicating the incense. "True," the clerk replies, a thin-haired man of fifty who looks like he is almost certainly still caught up in the music he listened to when he was much younger; he tells Aron that earlier this morning a young girl from Germany came into the store, bought a bunch of music, mainly Icelandic, and after completing her transaction asked him if she couldn't burn some incense, she felt the store lacked fragrance. He, the employee, did not know how to say no, especially since the girl had "saved the day" for the store with her purchases. "You know what it reminds me of?" asks Aron. "Let me guess," says the clerk, and mentions an English name that G. gathers is the name of a band. Aron says "What?" then adds "The smell reminds me of a girl I was once with. Or am with. What color was this German girl? I mean her hair." "Red, I think," replies the clerk. "You think?" Aron asks, laughing, and G. starts to sympathize with the follicly-challenged character, because there is hostility in Aron's laughter, and when a younger man needles an older, it can smart. Aron continues, adding that "redheads are the best." As he explains just what he means, G. once again recognizes his disgust for this person rising inside him. "So you *are* with this girl, or you *were* with her?" the clerk asks, like he is doing his best to follow this young man in what G. cannot consider anything but an inappropriate subject. "When *is* a man with some girl, and when *was* a man with her?" Aron replies. And when the clerk starts showing an affected interest in the topic, or perhaps an unconvincing one, from the sound of his reaction, Aron goes one step further, sharing something two people who have never talked to each before should share, and he tells the thin-haired clerk that he is heading to meet a girl later, that he is going to stay at her place tonight, but that does not mean he is *with* her. What does it mean, then? G. asks himself as he loiters over a similar collection of music to the box set he gave his mother and father, on a shelf above the rack where he is standing. The two men he is listening to, from here in the corner of this little store, seem in some way to get on rather well as they start exchanging the knowledge they think they possess about redheaded women, and as part of this topic their vocabulary becomes gradually more English rather than Icelandic. G. strives to hear every word that falls from their lips. And he reminds himself of the fact that Aron certainly had, when he was younger, known a redheaded woman, a fact that sorely wounds him each time he recalls it. He finds it, as before, a very unpleasant place for his mind to wander. In this moment, he wants above all to do something to Aron, even if only to throw him to the floor or punch him in the jaw, anything that will make clear to him, and not only him, but also anyone present to witness it, for example the clerk, that G. despises the values and beliefs he feels sure Aron holds dear. "If I were going to buy something from you," he hears Aron say, "what would you suggest, for a guy like me?" At once it occurs to G. that Aron is about to offer the clerk something for sale, if he in turn buys something in the shop; as he thinks it, he tries to hear for himself the sounds behind the names the clerk suggests to Aron. It does not surprise him in the least that the list includes the old folk singer G. himself had thought about in connection with the fence, the cognac drinking, and the violin. It does surprise him, however, that Aron considers the suggestion, though it won't be top of the list when it comes to choosing something to buy. G. never hears what ultimately gets chosen, but what undeniably sheds new light on Aron Cesar, in G.'s eyes, is that the former would prefer to buy vinyl and not a CD. G. had not imagined Aron having a turntable in his loft. He continues to listen to their chat, and feels his antipathy toward Aron flare again when the clerk somehow circles back to the topic of *redheaded women*. But then Aron thanks him, and they say goodbye to one another. Aron leaves the store. G. lets a little time pass before he too leaves, but as he walks past the counter, and the clerk asks, "All set?" it strikes G. that this thin-haired man, who does not seem to be a day under fifty, has been charmed by his conversation with the half-Brazilian. It is still raining when G. walks out of the store.

•

It is difficult to say whether what he feels toward this man, whom he has now pursued for almost two hours, is pure hatred. Is the feeling strong enough that he would go ahead and harm Aron, were he somehow given the opportunity? Yet Aron showed gratitude in the store, G. recalls as he follows him at a distance down Laugavegur and then onto Bankastræti. G. lets himself wonder whether the album Aron bought was a kind of private reward for his earlier transaction. To reward oneself for something that has not yet been achieved is something G. knows all too well. He uses the method all the time to motivate himself to do better, and it works. Because he could never live with receiving compensation for something he has not finished. The only thing that disturbs him in this respect is dying in the midst of an incomplete project for which he has already been remunerated. But would such a death not be a kind of payment?

•

The rain worsens. Aron turns off Bankastræti onto Bernhöfts-
torfustígur, and from there goes down the stairs and out onto
the little patch of grass behind the large statue of the woman
with water pails. If he was light of foot when he walked along
Laugavegur, after his business transaction in Þingholtsstræti, his
step is even lighter now, and has ample grounds for being so.
Trade flourishes, his mind has been refreshed with a beer, and
yet more beer is on the way, together with soccer on television;
he has acquired some new music, on shiny black vinyl, music undoubtedly already spinning revolutions in his head; and at the
end of the day the warm embraces of a woman—potentially a
redhead—await him. He transfers the plastic bag with his new
record over to the hand holding the umbrella, and uses the other
to slap the broad backside of the statue, on her ass, hitting rather
firmly, it seems, and aggressively. When he reaches the sidewalk
of Lækjargata he heads over to the front vehicle by the taxi sign,
taps on the passenger-side window, and puts down his umbrella.
Then he opens the door, says something to the driver, and stoops
inside. It's not possible to say whether G. had already made a
decision, but as soon as Aron let slip, during his phone call in
the record store, the words "take a cab," he felt that should not
discourage him from staying in the chase. G. tries to imagine the
next hours of his life, whether he has on his hands a long trip,
with the meter of the cab flickering mercilessly, whether he will
be forced to wait a long time in the cab while Aron meets the
man to whom he spoke before returning downtown to watch the
game. It's been a long time since G. was last in a taxi. But isn't

that all the more reason to explore this part of Aron's journey? Without giving the driver of the car behind any particular notice, G. opens the door and asks if he is free. Of course he's free, he's there waiting for passengers. He settles into the back seat and asks the driver, a young man with strikingly pale features, to pursue the car in front. The driver looks at him, puzzled, and then points to the car in front. "That one?" "Yes," says G. "Go when he goes." "But shouldn't you just go in the other car with him?" asks the driver with a smile. "Wouldn't it be cheaper for both of you to share a ride?" The question comes out of the blue; G. initially decides not to answer, but is forced to when the driver asks again. And he lets the wrong response slip out, giving the pale man at the wheel yet more of a motive to smile. No doubt G. isn't thinking entirely clearly at the moment, he isn't accustomed to such situations, getting into a taxi and asking the driver to follow the car in front. By the time he has fastened his seatbelt and looks up, out the window, he sees that Aron has exited his car. He waves to the driver and slams the door. G. releases his belt, but waits before getting out, wanting to let Aron decide where he should head next. As G. reckons he knows, Aron is on the way to the sports bar. But what had caused him to settle into a taxi only to emerge from it again one minute later? As soon as Aron heads toward the crosswalk, G. excuses himself, and asks if he owes the driver anything. The driver smiles like before, and shakes his head.

•

I'll send it by cab to your place later. That's what Aron had said on the phone, not *I'll take a cab to your place later*, like I heard him say.

•

Aron has almost reached the crosswalk to Lækjartorg Square by the time G. exits the car. But as he starts to hurry after him, G. hears the taxi driver call out: "Don't lose him!" G. spins around to look back at him, and the driver's pale face is halfway out the window. And he does not stop there: "Keep up with him!" the driver shouts, even louder than before. And it seems Aron can hear him, because he turns around. As does G., too, to avoid making eye contact with Aron. When G. looks back toward Lækjartorg, Aron still has his eyes on the taxi, and he himself is in the line of sight. Aron meets his eyes for a moment, a few moments. And G. can see that Aron is thoughtful, even surprised, by the driver's shouts. And conceivably by him, G., too, this man paused midway between Aron and the taxi. Is it a coincidence that I have seen this man in the black overcoat pop up more than once, more than twice, in the last two hours, G. imagines Aron wondering. But wouldn't he already have reacted, if he had the feeling someone was following him?

•

The Dandy? What he wouldn't give to know what was going through this fellow's head.

•

But what was the driver playing at? Does he think I owe him
something? G. ponders. Is he claiming payment for my holding
up his car? G. turns around in a semicircle, not knowing at all
where to go. He is on the traffic island, caught between lanes,
cars approaching behind him, and the only thing he can think to
do is get back over the street and flee for cover behind the statue
of the woman carrying water. He almost trips over the sidewalk,
such is his haste.

•

He cannot tolerate having to rush.

•

In the sanctuary of the broad woman bearing her pails, G. takes
the risk of looking around for Aron, but by then Aron has van-
ished, no doubt well on his way to the bar on Austurstræti. If he
had set off by taxi, Aron and he would probably have gone as far
as Hverfisgata, if that was where they were headed; this struck
G. as the likeliest outcome. But it was a good feeling not to have
gone anywhere. And to know where Aron was going to be for the
next two hours or so. The prospect of that space of time raised
a number of questions in G.'s mind, which he decides to ponder
from within the supermarket opposite the sports bar, the one they
had previously been in. There were seats to sit at in the window.

•

He avoids looking in the direction of the taxis as he crossed
Lækjargata, knowing that the pale driver's eyes will be scanning
the area for him.

•

But why is he doing this? He could be home listening to Jaroussky or Gérard Souzay singing Fauré or Hahn. Or Duparc. He
could have mailed his envelope. But instead he has gone into a
supermarket, actually little more than a glorified kiosk, gone into
it for a second time, this place where the music coming through
the speakers is controlled by some addled adolescent at a radio
station nowhere near here, in some other part of the city. He
is hungry. But now he can allow himself what he wanted back
when he watched Aron buy croissants, plums, and yogurt: to get
something himself. He decides he wants þykkmjólk, the sugary
yogurt drink. Croissants, two of them, one with ham and cheese,
the other plain. He also gets a coffee, but skips the plums. And
he sits down by the window, from where he has a view out onto
Austurstræti.

•

The sports bar. And not just the bar itself, but he can even see
Aron Cesar inside the bar, sitting at a table by the window. Someone is sitting opposite him, at the same table, it looks like they

are talking. Maybe it's his imagination, but G. feels that there is a sense of anticipation in the air inside the bar. He discerns this from the gestures of the various people moving to and fro inside. One of them touches a TV screen on the wall; another ferries three pints of beer over to one of the tables.

•

He arranges the croissants, yogurt drink, and the coffee cup so that the croissant with the ham is closest to him on the table. Behind it, the carton of þykkmjólk, and behind that, next to the window, the other croissant. He sets the coffee beside the carton, to its right, and he reaches out for a newspaper someone here before him has left open. Then he casts his eyes over a little story about a young chamber music group that is heading to the Baltic States to give a concert, accompanied by some dancers. What does dance have to do with chamber music? The music group has more girls than boys. More young women than young men. But are these youths old enough to be considered gentlemen? Chamber Gents. *Chamber Gents?* Where has that phrase come from? He knows that he read it in a novel, he remembers the book's cover being red. The ham-and-cheese croissant tastes amazing. It's a taste that reminds him especially of England, of the only trip he took overseas with his parents. He uses the past tense, not the continuous present, "he has taken," etc., because the three of them, he and his mother and his father, are not likely to travel together again. But he had recalled this earlier. He had gone to the city of Bath, in England, with them. He was

fifteen then, and they in their mid-sixties. This was one of two
international journeys he had taken in his life, the other being to
Paris eight years back; that time, he went alone. That trip he also
replays in his mind, sitting here watching Austurstræti, anticipat-
ing eating the other croissant, which he's planning to have with
his coffee.

•

He sips þykkmjólk along with his ham croissant. And he wonders again about the phrase *Chamber Gents*. What about men like
himself and Aron? Thirty-five years old, but each in his own way
not deserving to be called a gentleman, even less a chamber gent.
These young people who are on the way to the Baltic States to
play their classical instruments can, on the other hand, lay claim
to such a title, at least in the not-so-distant future, and perhaps
already. These kinds of people are accustomed to wearing, from
an early age, a hat and tails, as the saying goes; they've passed
all sorts of exams in this and that at high school and college, in
addition to all their musical degrees. He knows their type. Sara
had all the accoutrements of such a group, and would undoubtedly have made many trips like the one he's reading about in the
paper, had her life taken the direction her parents intended for
her. If he reads the press report correctly, these young, creative
folk are likely ten years or more younger than Aron. And what
about the two of them? They're both the age Mozart was when
he died. In this vein, he recollects the names of several artists
and poets who did not live longer than Mozart, but nevertheless

attained such success that he, sitting on a tall stool and looking out on Austurstræti, remembers their names. How could men like he and Aron Cesar possibly do something that left a mark? Will today contribute anything significant? In such a short time, it would be unlikely he could achieve anything of merit that others would notice; far easier to record one's name in history through something malevolent. Some evil. By stopping someone or other in their tracks. What he's reading at the moment, back at home, is a biography of a man whom he cannot wait to die between the covers of the book. Something on every page screams out to the reader's desire for the subject to be removed from play immediately, even though the reader knows it won't happen until the end of the book, on page six hundred something. What a monster this man was. I have already mentioned that nothing is more tedious than stories or conversations about crime and drugs, yet one thing that frustrates me more than drugs and crime is the man in the half-read book, the spiritual father to Mussolini in Italy, who gathered about himself beautiful things and beautiful women, radiating like the sun with his self-confidence, then defiled beauty by fucking her. Apologies. He had not meant to use such language. It was not in his nature. But he let it be, he let it feature. Sorry again, he had not meant to rhyme. But to have started reading a book, to have made a decision about a book you intend to read, ought to demand reflection and responsibility to one's nature. Going as far into a long book as he has done with the biography I just mentioned forces one to grasp for terra firma. There's no stopping mid-chapter. But he just cannot wait for the subject to die off. He wants to get the assurance at the book's close that this vile person is dead, even though he has already cheated by flicking through the final pages and scanning for what would be revealed in the final description, with the following words: ". . . dies from a stroke at his desk." But the assurance that he dies still cannot be obtained except by reading every word in the order it appears. And instead of staying home and reading, he is sitting here in a kiosk masquerading as a supermarket, and he has just been shouted after on the street.

•

. . . *by fucking her* . . . I wonder how I look in the eyes of the people walking past the screamingly huge window of the store? If they care to look at me, that is. *He defiled her by entering her* . . . Would these people suspect that the young man on the other side of the glass had never been inside another person? He had come out of his mother, and has not been anywhere since.

•

The second croissant is equally satisfying. He did not know he was so hungry. Neither did he think he had it in him to use the kind of words he had just been thinking. The smell of the croissant, and its taste, takes his mind to France, calls up images of his second trip abroad. And as he takes a sip of coffee he watches Aron Cesar get up from the table inside the sports bar.

•

He knows, he can see on the sports page of the newspaper in front of him, that today's match, the one which has dragged Aron inside the bar, is between England and Costa Rica. He wonders if his father is perhaps over at his nephew's, that coarse man who today is undoubtedly drunker than usual because England is in the spotlight. And because he knows his father has not returned from an errand he should long since have concluded, G. reckons it more than likely he ended up in the apartment with the giant screen, even though the German team is not playing. His mother would already have let him know if his father had showed up. But then she should already have called him to express concern that he still hadn't returned from the bakery. In other words, he expects a call from her shortly.

•

The trip to England with his elderly parents was actually one of the most ridiculous things he has ever heard of. What is there for a fifteen-year-old, a teenager, to do in Bath, England, totally alone with his middle-aged—well past middle-aged—parents, a man and a woman who had only had on their itinerary seeing some Roman monuments and visiting a bath where the Romans had once bathed? It was a totally dissimilar and enjoyable experience for the same person, twelve years later, to go on his own to the world's capital, a capital as far as he sees the world. Where he saw the pelican in the zoo. Where it saw him.

•

It approaches, it draws me the way a magnet attracts a needle. It looks for all the world like my darling redhead, my beloved.

•

Aron sits back at the table; he has gone to get himself a beer. But then he stands up and heads back to the bar, and returns to set another full glass on the table. Aron Cesar. I should maybe call him again.

•

It was on some bridge between the left and right banks of Paris, I cannot remember what the bridge was called, that I heard the voices of Icelanders. I have already mentioned I was twenty-seven at the time. Before I went abroad, I read a book I got at the library, by some Putnam, an American, where he's describing eight blond Icelanders in Paris during the third decade of the twentieth century, who every night faithfully went to a particular bar in Montparnasse, and never said a word to anyone else, but stood erect at the bar and drank themselves stiff, striding out into the night and going to their studios. According to the author of the book, they were artists. Since I'd just finished the book, this Putnam's description was fresh in my mind when I heard the voices of the two Icelanders on the bridge, and it came to light, after I followed my compatriots for a good part of the day, that one of them, the man in his seventies, tremendously mismatched to look at yet not disheveled, was some kind of artist. The other man, who was a little younger, possibly mid-fifties, seemed to me to be interviewing the older man; at least, he kept on asking questions and getting answers in between, and the conversation sounded like it concerned the life and career of the older man. Much of what I heard them say I recorded in my notebook when I returned to the hotel that evening. I had tracked them into a café, into a bar, and finally into a restaurant, until they disappeared into an apartment on the other side of the river, the right side, some kind of apartment block, very ugly and gray. Somehow I found out, I do not remember how, that this building was connected with some kind of arts organization. I guessed that the Icelanders, at least the elder one, the artist, had some space in the building, presumably a studio, like the blond Icelanders in the American book. A large part of their back-and-forth, the artist and the interviewer, was about some book that was seemingly going to be published by the artist's brother—who in fact they made much fun of—and that concerned the artist's career—but what struck me afterward as most memorable was their very peculiar conversation about the Nanga Parbat mountain in the Himalayas. It was obviously on the artist's agenda to create some work or other with Nanga Parbat in the title; he thought it was amusing, not least because the name Nanga Parbat, abbreviated, had the same initials as his own. I have yet to find out who these people were, or are; I tried to find out after I came home from Paris, but soon gave up. I do not know, therefore, whether the book they discussed was ever published or not.

•

The reason I dwell on this memory from Paris is, however, that after reading the news about the chamber group, I began to think about the manuscript in my bag, and to wonder about the response it would get from the people to whom it was addressed. Will it be considered by an editorial board? Or will it be only the publisher who runs his eyes over it, and allows his so-called daily disposition, the way he feels at that particular moment, dictate whether he reads beyond the first two or three pages? To send this off, away from me, to get it out of my hands, one might say that it is at the moment a half-finished work. And therefore simply initiated. Because all it has left is to reach its conclusion. But the course of events doesn't run ahead of a person, it does not give one the slip. It does not wait for you, either. I am sitting here in the building next to the post office, I could so easily uproot myself a moment, go next door, even leave my unfinished coffee for a little while. But I decide not to return to the post office before tomorrow, when I will come back with the letter my mother asked me to mail. She must be about to call me, any moment. But if it reaches the editors, those I imagine there in the building to which the envelope is addressed, and they examine the contents, what questions will they ask? "But what about the girl, the one mentioned at the outset? What happens to her?" I feel quite sure that will be the first question they ask themselves: "Does the man who crossed himself in the cemetery have nothing more to do with the story? And will something happen with the newly-sharpened knives of the restaurateur, Ugo, other than their being used to cut meat?" But I have not mentioned any knives, I will not take responsibility for them. Indeed, it is also not certain that these people, whom I imagine to be two or three women, and the publisher, a man, will have read the story in its entirety when they discuss the manuscript. Perhaps they will have gotten no further than the point where I have the publisher himself say: "But why is he pondering the publisher's response? Should he not instead be worrying about the reader?" And when the two women, or three, agree, the publisher adds a third question: "Why doesn't he just continue with the story?"

Half an Hour Later

And that's what he does. He continues. The match between the English and Costa Rican national teams begins about a quarter of an hour after G. settles into the sports bar. It is much brighter in the Brazilian stadium than the stage they find themselves on, he and Aron. But there is much merriment here. The atmosphere is relatively calm and well-tempered, considering an important match is at stake, something that traditionally involves fights or brawls, especially among spectators. G. sits with three young men at a table next to Aron; he gets their permission, he does not barge in on them. Aron has his back to him, and although he turns to follow the game on the television screen, to which he in fact doesn't devote much attention, it is unlikely that Aron notices him. G. however, recognizes another man he knows, or at least has often seen, and not only recently or over a span of years, but almost all his life. This fifty-something man lives in Vesturbær, the west part of town, somewhere close to Aragata, possibly on Lynghagi or Fálkagata; he's a rather singular character, one of his neighborhood's landmarks, you could say. As far back as G. can remember, back to the first time he saw this man, from around the end of elementary school up through G.'s high-school years, the man wore blue. Always blue, except his footwear. G. is amazed, thinking about it, that he never managed to learn the man's name. He cannot remember exactly why, but at some point his mother mentioned this person, and they talked about the jacket he wore, a so-called reporter's jacket, an item of clothing reminiscent of a soldier's uniform due to its many deep pockets, an indication that whoever was wearing the garment had all kinds of things on their person, plenty to keep them busy. G.'s mother once actually wanted him to have this kind of jacket, wanted to buy it for him at the Uniform Store on Laugavegur, after his father had advised her that such jackets were on sale there. As soon as G. recalls his parents' peculiar suggestion that he wear a particular item of clothing, one they wanted to give him, he is surprised to realize, once again, how little interest they typically showed in him. Is it an ugly thought that the money he receives from them by way of monthly allowance is compensation for accepting their apathy? Wouldn't it have sufficed to point this jacket out to him at the Uniform Store, wasn't there some dogged affectation involved in wanting to get it for him? G. has enough money himself, money he gets from them. He

declined the jacket. A reporter's jacket is not for him. He is not a
journalist. And on that note, there is no way the blue-clad man,
the one present now, inside the sports bar on Austurstræti, has a
job reporting the news to people. At first glance, he's not watching the game, sitting alone at a table further inside the place, a
beer in front of him, deep in thought. G. casts his mind back
about twenty years. He is standing at the high school's west door,
looking toward the cathedral tower of Neskirkja. Above him, the
sky, the clear sky of memory; he has no idea why he puts it so
poetically, given that he never felt comfortable at school. The
blue man comes walking along the pavement, tromping in the
direction of Hagatorg, no doubt on his way downtown, and one
of G.'s school friends, whom G. thinks it ridiculous to consider a
friend, points at the man, who back then would have been about
thirty years old, maybe just over, and says something to the effect
that he would not want to run into this guy in the dark. The blue
man's stooping gait, the way he seems to press his foot hard and
determined against the ground with each step, used to draw the
attention of the kids as he passed. G. remembers that one of his
peers, whom he finds it odd to call a peer, like calling the other
kid a friend, wrote a short story that won some competition at
school, and the man in the reporter's jacket was a character in
the story, his role being to follow a young girl home from prom.
The story did not end well, he remembers that much, and he
also remembers having felt that such stories should not be written. But such stories are always being written, more often than
they actually happen in reality. I think, on the other hand, that
in actuality, on this rain-soaked June day, the blue man has not

come here to watch the World Cup. Because that's not what he is doing. He is doing something altogether different. He *is* some place altogether different. And, thinking along those lines, I recall a phrase from one of the two books my parents' former tenant left in my apartment when he moved out, those books I have made my own: "And thus he is not *what* he is, he is *where* he is." And I see these two men before me, the tenant who formerly owned the books and the blue man, as the same person. These are people who somehow hang outside the center of existence, getting evicted from a rented apartment when someone else needs to use it, then landing the role of a violent man in some kid's prize-winning story, because no one knows what they are dealing with in reality.

•

He can hear that Aron has started talking on the phone. The person sitting opposite him seems to have his eyes glued to the screen on the wall. Aron does not. He apparently takes the call with some excitement, saying he was waiting to hear from the caller. "Listen," says Aron, and allows the word a little time to resonate, as though important information will follow on its heels. "You remember the boy who . . ." But then he lowers his voice, and his next words struggle against the sports bar's sound-scape, the murmur from the crowd at the game in Brazil, the forced excitement of the Icelandic commentator. G. gets the feeling all of a sudden that the boy Aron has mentioned must be him. G. That he *is* him. Aron's glance in Lækjargata, when he looked toward the cab, and then toward G., still haunts him; he thinks he knows that Aron is reporting over the phone that he saw him, and heard the driver shouting at him, like he, the "boy," was making a mess, had perhaps failed to pay his fare after the meter started running. "What was his name again?" G. hears Aron ask. He, Aron, has raised his voice once more. But then he returns to whispering, and something happens in the game that elicits a reaction from the audience. G. manages to hear, none-theless, that Aron agrees with the answer his interlocutor gives as to the "boy's" name; they have settled the matter. Then he stops talking on the phone. But what happens after the call? Does Aron turn to him and smile? No. He gets up to fetch another drink. One more beer. Number four, if not five. Aron then obvi-ously makes sure not to look in his direction when he returns to the table with the pint glass.

•

A goal is almost scored. Or so G. thinks he hears. The atmosphere in the place seems to be coming close to what is expected: things will come to a head, someone in here will pick any plausible rea-son to start a fight, a war of words at least—but just as suddenly as it looks like his wish will get fulfilled, there's a sudden silence. He was rather hoping to witness some kind of commotion. He looks at Aron out the corner of his eyes, trying to see if Aron is perhaps watching him, but cannot see any sign to indicate Aron is even tempted to look his way. Perhaps it's not surprising; he has had him in his sights long enough already, been aware of his presence long enough; no need to trouble himself. But what is Aron going to do? Is he expecting a continuing pursuit? Is he perhaps hoping for that? Is he even planning to start some kind of game? Some kind of chase? Cat and mouse? Mouse and cat? G. thinks it likely that Aron Cesar would look forward to such a thing. And following that thought, G. decides that Aron should get what he wants. But then, as he contemplates Aron from the back, he considers it more likely that everything he's interpreted as an indication of Aron's awareness of him, that Aron knows G. is following his every step, is actually nothing but fantasy.

•

The boy. "You remember him . . ." *Him,* the man who, today, this gray June day, in the middle of the Brazilian World Soccer Championship, has left his nest on Aragata, the street of intellectuals, and so given anyone who wants it the opportunity to reach into the living room window on the garden side, which G. knows he left open, just like the window in the back yard on Seltjarnarnes had been; by loosening the screws on the window clasp, anyone could creep in, open the door to the quiet street, relax in the calm as he removes all the furniture, rugs, and pictures that G. has gathered around himself—all without his mother, there on the upper floor, suspecting a thing, since the room where she spends her days faces out to the garden on the east side.

•

He overestimates this man, Aron Cesar. Why should he remember anything? And then to be confident someone has had the ridiculous idea of pursuing him. Placing himself in Aron's shoes, he finds it highly unlikely that he would be able to pretend nothing was amiss, if he knew another man was tailing him. What happens next, however, what comes to G's attention next, is that he notices the blue man watching him. Staring at him. Focused. G. allows himself to think that maybe this is an involuntary stare, which naturally doesn't involve much concentration, but when he looks away for a moment, and then looks back again, the latter still has eyes on him. He reaches for his glass, without taking his eyes off him, and it is as if the very stars have stopped moving while he takes a sip of beer. G. looks away again. He lets a few moments pass before he looks at him again. But now it's like the blue man had never noticed him. The way he looks straight past him, toward the door, leads G. to conclude that the guy's line of sight, which G. had felt certain was directed at him, in fact passed him by, that the blue man has been thinking about something that concerns him alone, which nothing outside his inner focus computed. And then there's some rising excitement in the game. And abruptly it comes to nothing; it was really nothing in the first place. The same pattern repeats itself immediately. And so nothing happens, twice. He cannot remember where the words come from, that nothing happens twice, but they are not unwelcome at this moment, which endures until they leave the scene, Aron and G.

•

"There's nothing doing," he hears one of the soccer fanatics say, when the crowd has persisted into the second half of the game and still no goal has been scored. It is not until Aron begins to speak into his phone again that anything happens, at least from his standpoint. G. in fact notices that the blue man occasionally sneaks a glance at him, but never again gets the impression that he's interested in him. Almost as soon as Aron's phone rings, his own phone does. But it only rings once, not long enough for him to answer it. He immediately suspects it was his mother; it is not the first time she has let him know, with one or two rings, that she is about to call him, like the ghost that knocks at the front door before the real guest arrives. And he's correct. She calls again two to three minutes later, right at the same moment as Aron says goodbye to whomever he is talking to, having gotten some information from him, a review, of some French film in the movie theater on Hverfisgata.

•

"Hi, Mom," G. says. If she only knew how he hesitates to use his full name. But she does not even greet him; there is something too important weighing on her chest for her to be able to do so. And all the while he is listening to her barrel on about his father, how worried she is about him, no longer because she doesn't know where he is, but now precisely *because* she knows where he is, he can hear Aron saying on the phone: "I can't be bothered to finish watching this game." Then he continues, saying he could just as well go to the movies, and why not, to see this French one, he recognizes one of the actors in it, someone only named on the other end of the line, and consequently he says to his conversation partner: "Blast from the past? A little like *Caligula*? No? But from the same era? Okay. But I'll blame you." He then confirms his interest in seeing the movie by adding that he would very much like to disappear into darkness for two hours, before going to visit . . . G. cannot follow what Aron says, because someone in the bar shouts something at the game, not to mention that his attention is occupied by his mother who is raising the idea of sending the police to find his father. Still, it is clear from the phone conversation that Aron is getting ready to leave. As soon as G. perceives from his mother that some mess has come up involving his father, and as soon as it's clear to him that he doesn't understand what the problem is, given that his father is precisely where his mother knows him to be, he decides to step out of the bar to talk to her outside. It is not raining at the moment, and he can simply wait outdoors for Aron to continue on his way. He looks over at the blue man, and half thinks about telling his mother that the man in the reporter's jacket is here under the same roof as him, although it might be said that the aforementioned is under his own roof right now, so deep in thought does he seem to be, with his eyes practically glued to the empty glass in front of him. "Wait a minute, Mom," says G., and gets up to go outside.

•

When his mother asks him about his movements, about where he is right now, he feels like she's occupied with something bigger. He places himself in the doorway one over from the post office, a building that houses an assortment of business offices. From here, he can watch the door of the sports bar. While he listens to his mother repeat her narrative about how his father is in the house of his nephew, the son of his brother, G. sees a twenty-something youth come out of the bookstore opposite; he pays attention to him because he has a man-bag not unlike his own—not only that, but the boy has a large-size envelope he has obviously bought from the store, and that is only lacking an address on it. Unlike G. himself, this young man has a patchy beard, and for some reason it's the beard itself that leads G. to reluctantly accept the fact that the boy is in front of him in line with his envelope; it would never occur to G. to let such a growth cover his features. "What do you think he told me, that good-for-nothing, your cousin?" His mother took every opportunity she got to avoid using his cousin's name. "He kept repeating that your dad was a real hot shot," she says. "And you can imagine how those words sound coming from the mouth of a man who hasn't left his couch in years. *Hot shot!*" Then she tells G. that he, the cousin, who is named Héðinn, had phoned to let her know that his father had come to visit him before noon, and they were now watching the World Cup match. And Héðinn had gone on about how G.'s father was such a hot shot, though to be honest he'd gotten a little sleepy, but he would definitely wake up again soon. His father was, in other words, drunk. He was dead drunk. And it was barely midday, just past. "But why would he call and tell me this?" G.'s mother shouts despairingly into the phone. G. agrees with her, but reacts by himself asking a question that he also feels needs directing to his mother: "But why are you telling *me* this?" "Am *I*?" she says. She hadn't expected that. "And Mom. Don't go phoning anyone else about this," he says. "But I'm talking about your father," she says, and G. reiterates to her that she must hold off on calling the police, as she had mentioned doing at the beginning of the call. "I don't think you have anything to worry about." Then he adds: "I'm also a bit busy at the moment." "*Also?*" she asks, astonished. "Busy? With what?" "I'll tell you later," answers G. "But I managed to buy the cream you told me to." "I don't think I ask you to do too much," says his mother, her voice sounding hurt, and he tries to convince her that he was not trying to imply that about having to go to the pharmacy for her. "Am I not your mother?" she continues, and at that moment he gets the impression that she is relieved to be talking about something other than his father. "I made you," she says. G. frankly does not know how to respond. And it seems his mother herself is surprised by these words; a shared silence enters their conversation. "I'll mail the letter for you tomorrow," says G. "In fact, I have to go to . . ." "And your father, of course, too," interjects his mother. "Dad what?" he asks. "It wasn't just me who made you," she says, slightly embarrassed. "Couldn't you look in on him?" she continues, meaning he should go to his cousin's. "No, Mom," he says. And as he repeats that he is busy, he sees the door of the sports bar open, and Aron emerge. Hot on his tail comes the blue man, as though they have departed together, have decided to leave as one. Which is altogether unlikely. G.

tells his mother that he has to hang up now, and allows himself to be somewhat brusque. He regrets it at once, and promises to call her back soon.

•

Aron takes a route directly to Lækjargata, and is obviously in a hurry. I see the blue man watch him go, but it quickly becomes clear they did not leave the bar together, not in the sense I first thought. I for my part set off as Aron approaches the corner of the District Courthouse. The confidence that characterizes his gait evaporates when he is hurrying like this.

•

How often must they have gone to the movies together, Aron and Sara. Back then, the movie theater on Hverfisgata had a different name, and G. imagines the rapidly-walking Aron is recalling memories of movies past. G.'s thoughts unexpectedly give way as another person crosses his path, a person intimately associated with Aron, although G. doesn't understand the connection immediately. As Aron surges past the District Courthouse toward the corner of Hverfisgata and Lækjargata, G. sees three middle-aged women in the middle of the square, walking north, virtually right in front of Aron, and he recognizes one of their faces at once, connecting her right away to Aron. Strange how the mind operates at moments like this, when two things collide before your eyes, things you know are linked, though can't think how, and before you can dredge up the link there comes a feeling that you have a duty to bring people together, because they are not capable of it themselves, they don't notice one another. It takes G. a few moments to realize that the woman he recognizes is Aron's mother. She's wearing a long rain- or wind-jacket, and along with the other two women is striding on at no less a pace than her son. Later, when he has managed to connect a name to the face, he feels like she must have seen her son walking there, practically in their way. So why didn't she do something? Did she not want to see him? He could hardly just pass her by. He was right in front of her, as close as when he, newborn, lay on her breast. To G.'s mind the coincidence is downright remarkable, that the mother of the man he has pursued since lunchtime should cross his path now, just when he, the son, is about to bring him, G., into the night, into the darkness of a movie theater, on one of Reykjavík's dingiest streets. Earlier today, when his own mother asked him if he had seen this woman in town, this former member of parliament, Ósk Völundardóttir, he indicated that he had. Could it be that his lie had been an omen, a sign he was going to see her a little later? His eyes follow her as she drifts away toward Hafnarstræti. She has dashed south, from Húsavík or Dalvík, he imagines, and that's why she is in such haste. She needs to conduct some business before heading back north. Aron himself has reached Lækjargata. G. takes care not to lose sight of him. But then, as he continues to look after Ósk, something happens that is no less strange. She looks briefly over her shoulder, not toward her son, but toward him. She has seen something that catches her attention. It must be that, since she allows herself a moment to look back. But only an instant. Perhaps to verify what she saw. Then they continue their rapid march, she and her two acquaintances, and soon disappear onto Hafnarstræti.

•

But was it him, G., whom she saw? Would she recognize his face from when she ran into him outside Parliament so many years ago? G. tries to picture for himself how things went between her and Sara when Aron first presented his girlfriend. Whether they became friends. And what impact it had on Ósk Völundardóttir, what happened later. Did she too experience the rug being pulled from under her son's feet? Start to cry?

•

One long-forgotten memory gets in G.'s way as he follows Aron up Hverfisgata, as they approach the National Theater. There, he remembers seeing Sara through the window of the bookshop opposite the theater, sometime during high school, at the beginning of his life's formless period, back when Aron and Sara were together. And he recalls struggling to decide whether he should go into the store, act like he had some reason to be there, casually bump into Sara. He did not do so. He didn't wade in. Because he usually doesn't wade in. He regrets this now, more than fifteen years later. Something could have happened. Sara might have

had a book in hand, and he would have pretended to know the
book, or actually would have known it, he had recently finished
reading it. He could have warned her off it. And she would be
grateful. Where, then, would Sara be today? The basement-level
second-hand bookstore is still there; indeed, the sign makes clear
it is open limited hours. But what about the violin he stole from
Sara's parents' window? Didn't he allow himself to wade in that
time? He did something no one, least of all he himself, might
have expected he would. Doesn't the same situation prevail now?
Isn't he allowing himself to wade in now, forging onward after
an ex-boyfriend of the girl he loved, up the dingiest street in the
city, focused on keeping up with him? Aron picks up his pace as
he draws closer to the movie theater. Aron is like G.; he does
not want to miss the first minutes of the movie. Because a movie
without the first minute, what is it but a story without a trigger?
Sun without shadow.

·

As G. stands at the entrance to the movie theater, on the steps
outside the door, he sees the blue man again. And he starts. But
he isn't sure whether this breeds unpleasantness, as is usual when
one startles. It is conceivable that he does not feel the slightest
bit bothered about seeing this man in the distance. All the same,
he makes sure not to look too long. But did the blue man see
him? Where exactly was he situated? On the corner of Vatnsstígur. He was standing there like a picture of a person, a figure cut from a plastic sheet and set on a cardboard background.

This brings to G.'s mind the old prints his father had showed him back when G. was ten or eleven years old, realistic images of famous battles and events in human history, which the polymath himself had pottered away at setting up according to his whim, imprinting figures with pencil onto colorful cardboard. His father had bought these pictures from an old classmate, the owner of a toy shop downtown, which G. remembers being on the corner of Bankastræti and Smiðjustígur. G. briefly finds this funny. He imagines that it had been his father who arranged the blue man there on the corner of Vatnsstígur and Hverfisgata, in the same kind of jacket that he, his father, had found in the so-called Uniform Store, and wished his son owned.

•

After Aron has finished buying his ticket, and G. is safe to enter the cinema, he looks back down Hverfisgata, by which time the blue man has disappeared. He pictures him having crossed over the street and gone down Skuggahverfi, rather than up Vatnsstígur toward Laugavegur. It occurs to G. that it had been his mind, not his eyes, which produced the image of Aron's mother a few minutes ago. In just the same way, the image of the blue man had been created. Printed pictures. For a moment G. thinks of the music store on Laugavegur, and he imagines the blue man browsing through the CDs. Is it conceivable that the blue man traveled with Aron and G. further than out of the sports bar? Unlike his father's cardboard pictures from the toy store, the background behind Aron and the blue man on this overcast

June day is not particularly colorful, but the color of the figures is, nonetheless, sufficiently vivid that they can easily be distinguished from one another, their outlines altogether different. G. watches Aron buy some refreshments. He stands by the ticket window and tries to pass the time by learning about the French movie he is going to see. Relative to the amount of refreshments Aron buys himself, it wouldn't hurt for him to be wearing a jacket like the blue man wears, with enough pockets to fit the Coke and beer bottle, the bag of popcorn and candy that the cashier has set out on the table in front of him.

•

G. is able to find out that the film, called *La Grande bouffe*, is a forty-year-old Italian-French production; these weeks are feature weeks showing old European movies, and this particular film has been specially selected for the schedule due to its numerous challenges. "Challenges from whom?" asks G., and the kid working there finds the question funny, answering with a smile: "From the middle-aged men who saw the film back in the day in the University Movie Theater." And when he mentions "Monday movie" at the University Movie Theater, G. recalls how his father told him about the tradition of movie-going in their part of town; what's more, he remembers, too, his mother's disapproval of the phenomenon, how she snorted when her husband, the philologist, recollected some Polish or Russian movies he'd seen on a Monday. G. sees before him the black-and-white darkness of the giant hall that was the University Movie Theater. And he pictures the blue man disappearing in there some thirty years ago. After he has paid for his ticket he waits for Aron to move away from the concession stand so that he can go over there himself. He does not have to wait long. He watches Aron tread carefully, with his acquisitions, toward the screening room. Coke and beer. G. noticed that Aron spent considerable time seasoning his popcorn. And did so considerably well, it seemed to him. Before he goes over to buy something to take into the screening room, he walks over to the front door and looks around, to see if he sees the blue man. It's started raining again. And everything is washed in gray. Which is good, he thinks, because that will add to the experience of settling into a dusky hall and watching colors flicker across the screen. He knows that the picture is in color, not black and white; he asked about that. And as he was asking, he thought of his father, of the movie trips they took together on Thursday evenings when his mother hosted her sewing circle. He was beside his father, at the ticket booth in the University Movie Theater, a ten- or twelve-year-old boy, his father sixty, in his woolen coat, asking the woman at the box office whether or not the movie was in color. It was his joke, to get his son to smile. "Yes, it's in color," said the boy in the box office. "But it only has English subtitles." But are there any nude scenes in it? G. had thought he should ask the boy, because that question had always burned on his lips when father and son went to the movies together.

•

Once he's inside the room, and can see Aron is sitting near the center of one of the front rows, his head casting a small shadow onto the very bottom edge of the screen. G. suddenly has the desire to go over to him and tell him that he saw his mother just now. The top of Aron's head against the screen is like a page number at the bottom of a white page in a book, or would be if the screen were white. But it is not: a trailer for some recent Icelandic movie is being projected on it. In addition to Aron and himself, there are three people in the theater: two sitting together in the middle, and the third toward the end of the row behind Aron. All men. G. sits in the next-to-last row, further in. At that point, his phone rings. And he asks himself, as he opens up the handset, why his father never calls him, whether a call from his father would not have some major significance to him at that moment. But, as before, his mother is on the line. From her nervous agitation, G. at first supposes a worse fate has befallen his father than overstaying at Héðinn's, or being called a hot shot, but it's something else entirely: G.'s mother letting him know that his father did finally return home. "Good," he says, and starts to explain to her that he unfortunately can't talk right now. But he does not get far, because his mother interrupts him. "I'm not going to tell you what he looked like," she says, disapprovingly. "He took a cab home. And his shirt covered in ketchup, or I don't know what. Blood, perhaps? He was simply in no condition to tell me himself. And the taxi driver didn't know anything." "Mom, I'm at the movies," G. cuts her off, and decides right away to add, to mend things, that he's at the movies with a young man he met today. She reacts by saying his name, as if with an exclamation mark after it, and that leads G. to think about giving a name to this imaginary person he has mentioned, giving him a name chosen from those scrolling over the movie screen as part of the trailer for the Icelandic movie currently being shown. But he lets suffice the explanation that "this guy" he met has dragged him along to some French film. But his mother does not believe him. "Are you with a girl?" she asks. And G. asks himself: Does she think it's Sara? Does she perhaps suspect her son has lost all touch with reality, that he is telling a lie about the guy because he is embarrassed that he is imagining Sara sitting next to him in the theater? Or does his mother not remember what happened to Sara? Did she ever know? "No, Mom, there's no girl," he says. "You can tell me," she replies, and it is as if she is worried she will not get to see her little boy again. "Be careful that Dad doesn't sleep on his back," he says. "He's sleeping," she says. But when G. promises to call her later, and repeats the words a little louder, because she cannot hear him, he is shouted at by other moviegoers: "Quiet down back there!" That's Aron, he can tell. And Aron turns around in his seat, staring back for a few moments.

•

G. tells his mother he will call her at intermission. He turns off the phone by depressing the red button for a few seconds. As soon as the light on the screen turns off, he remembers he has forgotten the code needed to turn the phone on again, a number that is written on his calendar at home. He also remembers that the Hverfisgata movie theater doesn't have intermissions. What awaits him is an uninterrupted movie, a phone gone dark.

And a Little More Than One Hundred Minutes Pass

As he pursues Aron out of the screening room, there's about a quarter of an hour remaining in the movie. That the half-Brazilian should have asked for quiet before the movie started is, in retrospect, rather paradoxical, given he was the one gesticulating and yelling during the feature, practically the whole time, as soon as it became clear to him he disliked the movie; in reality, it was admirable how long he allowed himself to watch it. Before the scene that finally caused Aron to stand up and walk out, G. had already decided to see this film again, as soon as possible. From the first minute, he felt he belonged in this movie's world and, what's more, as well as feeling that he was part of the opulence and finery adorning the scenes, he felt his father somehow belonged to the group of four men the story followed. Or, rather, he ought to. In short, he had never had such an intense movie experience. And, in fact, it is ridiculous that he leaves to follow Aron out before the movie ended. Aron doesn't deserve it. And that's why he thinks to himself, as he quits the room, he will ask the box office clerk on the way out whether there's another showing tomorrow. But as he walks toward the lobby in the shadows of the theater, his eyes following Aron's back as he approaches the front door, he sees the blue man sitting at a table in the café. And even though this time the image of the man is made of flesh and blood, and not anything like the prints his father got from the toy shop, the first thing that comes to G.'s mind is the word *imagined.*

•

But he is not imagined. He is sitting there. With a cup of coffee in front of him on the table. He is looking toward the box office, and G. can see his eyes follow Aron when the latter goes out the door, heading into the rain. The blue man has a baseball cap on his head, red and yellow. It's a hat with the movie theater logo on it; he must have bought it at the concession stand. It occurs to G. to take a little detour on his way out, so as to avoid the blue man seeing him, but aside from the fact that there's no way to make a detour, since the only exit is on the same side as the ticket booth, deep down G. actually wants this man to see him. He feels again the sensation that seized him two hours ago, that it's not a bad thing the blue man is following them. As soon as Aron has left his sight, G. looks back toward the box office, but he cannot tell whether the blue man sees him go past. He decides not to stop to ask about the next showing of the movie or if there is even going to be one, since he can find that out later. He does not want to lose Aron, who undoubtedly is now halfway up Frakkastígur. He seems to be making a beeline for somewhere. G. looks over his shoulder as he emerges outside, but cannot see if he is being followed by the blue man, who seems to be as before, his eyes on the box office. And G. steps down to the sidewalk. It's raining. Now with the same intensity as in the morning. G. raises his umbrella, but waits to open it, because he sees Aron turning right, at the corner of Frakkastígur. He must keep up with him. He thinks he knows for sure where Aron is heading, and if he is right, then there is barely any point in opening up the umbrella, because he would have to close it again only moments later to enter the place he has in mind: a bar on Frakkastígur, in the middle of a row of houses that extend up to Laugavegur. This is a tavern that suits Aron, he thinks. Even more than the pub earlier.

•

He's intuited right. Aron goes into the tavern. But what is it like inside? G. has never been there before, only fabricated an image of the place in his mind after seeing, at some point, a few of the clientele gathered on the pavement outside, shivering with their cigarettes and glasses in the bitter cold. But as soon as he stands at the open door, the first thing that comes to him is that people

are surely allowed to smoke in here. The pungent stench crashes
into his face, mixed with rather old-fashioned rock music, Icelandic, which he feels is surely being played and sung by dead-
drunk men, perhaps because it's being drowned out by the crowd
noise on the television from the World Cup in Brazil. Neither
the music nor the soccer are set especially loud, but this strange
mix of sound causes G. to miss the bewitching and sophisticated
music that accompanied the movie a few moments ago, music
Michel, one of the four gentlemen in the house in Paris, played
on the piano, wearing a light pink turtleneck, and Marcello, in
his white cable-knit cardigan, put on the record player on another occasion. The charismatic melody Michel played again on the
piano, just before he died on the balcony, is not only something
G. knows he will remember for the rest of his life; he sees the
notes before him, as if they are physical entities, tiptoeing after
him, first at a normal tempo, then picking up the pace, like they
did with Michel: the notes running faster than their legs can
manage, tangling themselves up.

•

But is he coming after him, the blue man, in his reporter's jacket?
G. looks back down Frakkastígur, but does not see him. On the
contrary, sauntering up the sidewalk come three rather heavy
and serious men, the sort to have been hitting the streets for a
while now, and there is no doubt that they are on the way into
the same place as him. One of them is wearing a similar coat as

two of the bankers he saw disappearing into the fast food place at lunchtime. Now the coats of the bankers are hanging in suburban closets, he thinks, alongside nylon parkas, sports jackets, and knee-length anoraks with leather buttons; now the bankers are eating their dinners in their houses under the shadow of their clocks, clocks which show it's dinnertime. G. goes into the bar. And he shakes the water from himself, like a cat.

•

The semi-darkness inside makes him recall the darkness of his phone. And he tries to assess the urgency in calling his mother, like he promised. Would they have a public telephone in a place like this? Didn't his mother call that sort of phone a ten-króna-phone? If someone was at home in his apartment waiting for him, he would simply call the person and ask her to go to his calendar on the living room table to find the code that would unlock the cellphone. But there's no one to mobilize in the building on Aragata but his mother, up there on the top floor, and his sleeping father, who is now presumably on his back, done-in, as G. imagines Aron phrasing it. He can hardly call his mother to get her assistance turning on his phone, only so he can call her back. He walks up to a young woman sitting at the end of the bar, wearing an apron around her waist, and so likely employed there. He asks her if they have a telephone. She points toward the restrooms, and says she thinks the phone on the wall in front of the toilet still works. But where is Aron? Possibly he has gone to the toilet. Aron whom, given his reaction to the movie, G. had expected ten minutes ago would yell out in terror when the toilet in the Parisian house exploded, with the worst possible consequences. It was a really creepy scene, one of the darkest he's experienced in a movie. But he smiled as he watched it. He laughed internally. He may even have laughed out loud. Because something inside him opened up, seeing the toilet erupting the way it did, spewing out of itself everything that was meant to go down into the earth. But from Aron all he heard was silence. He had, to put it plainly, been rendered speechless, he thinks. And for the rest of the film the stench of the toilet lay over the house. It was not until Michel expired on the balcony railing shortly after that G again heard from the half-Brazilian, so stricken he seemed to be over the exploding toilet.

•

Ugo, Philippe, Marcello, and Michel. Those gentlemen once again become vivid in G.'s mind as he recalls them. Philippe, the owner of the building in Paris; Michel, the one who blew up the toilet. He has yet to see what becomes of Ugo and Philippe, what their fate will be by the end of the film. But why didn't he stay in the movie theater? Shouldn't he have rather walked toward the screen than away from it? This in turn leads him to wonder why a forty-year-old European film has such a harsh effect on someone of Aron Cesar's temperament. Should it not rather have had that effect on G. himself?

•

But what were the names of the individuals holed up here, in this bar on Frakkastígur? Is Eddi, Aron's friend, hidden somewhere in the depths of all this darkness? He notices a man sitting at the bar, a man of about forty, in some kind of distinctive uniform, a jacket with epaulettes, and he feels like this man must be called Sævar. Or Garðar. This man knows the guys who enter the place after G., the men he saw walking up the street. While G. chooses a seat near the bar he watches these same men "survey" their everyday surroundings, as he describes it to himself; the everyday is certainly in full force inside here, as well as outside. A rainy wet Tuesday in late June, and the World Cup tournament about halfway over. He thinks so, at least. It turns out that these men also know Aron, though they all seem to be considerably older than him. Because when Aron comes out of the toilet, he stops at the bar to chat with them, some kind of reunion. G. hears Aron mention the name of the movie theater on Hverfisgata. Indeed, he believes he hears some numbers mentioned, and speculates that the debate at the bar has turned to the purchase and sale of whatever Aron has to offer. But the conversation quickly goes back to focus on the movie, and there is general laughter. Then Aron orders a beer. And a shot of something; G. doesn't hear what. Aron then takes out his phone and walks away from the bar, toward the front door, while he is waiting for it to be answered.

•

Here I am before all of you . . . But G. is seated; there's no way you could describe him as "before" or in front of everyone, for the main advantage of this particular meeting place is undoubtedly that it allows you to be solitary . . . *a man full of good sense knowing life and death* . . . Being in a dive like this reveals that you know nothing, neither about life nor death, though G. feels he has gotten a little insight into the two worlds from the hundred minutes he spent in the movie theater . . . *with gloved hands I let life go* . . . Something to that effect was a line of a poem by Corbiére; he thinks he has remembered it right. *In my distastes above all I have elegant tastes. You know that with gloved hands I let life go* . . . Michel had orange rubber gloves on his hands when he lifted up to the sky the pig's head from the butcher's truck. *Le nouveau style*, as he described the gloves in the beginning of the film, taking them from the packet to try them on. *Plus sensibles*. Elastic and durable. *Le nouveau style*.

•

"Where did you send me!" he hears Aron shout into the phone. "*Blast from the past?* What were you even thinking?" Aron moves back closer to the bar, to get his drinks, and he sees the man in uniform pass the shot glass in his direction, the one Aron ordered, but the other man whips it quickly away at the next moment, with a mischievous expression, and knocks it back. And grimaces. Then waves to the bartender, and asks for another shot. And he laughs a forced laugh. G. understands at this moment that the names that he tried out for this man together form the name of the street Sara lived on, in the garden house behind her parents' home. Sævargarðar, out in Seltjarnarnes. Where the violin disappeared from the window. Where the married couple's social gathering on the promontory got so wild that the housewife's violin lay forgotten on the windowsill. It was at an altogether more elegant place than this one here on Frakkastígur that he later negotiated a price for the instrument. How large had the amount been? Was it not further proof of his parents' general indifference that they never asked any questions about their son's increased income? The transaction took place in a hotel, not far from Laugardalur. Helpfully, the buyer didn't live in this country. G. remembers the proceeds being enough for his two dining chairs, his bookcase with glass doors, a smoking table, a chaise longue and console table, and, last but not least, the Indian secretary at which he wrote. And there was still a considerable amount left. *So easy to look at, so hard to define.* He can still taste the brandy from the bottle, the memory still satisfies any need he has for an alcoholic drink, he can even still feel the rigid fence-post against his back, and the soft texture of the instrument. If it is right that the past is a foreign country, then he does not want to live there.

•

There's no evidence that Aron lets the behavior of the uniformed man get on his nerves; rather, he is busy talking on the phone. "Why would you think I'd have a good time?" he says, shocked, and gets loud encouragement from Sævar-or-Garðar, "Let him have it!" And then he has a new shot in his hand. Aron holds the phone to his ear with his shoulder, and walks with his two glasses across to the next table over from G.'s own. "Luckily I wasn't born when this abomination was made," says Aron as he sits down, just as shocked as before, but now laughing. "What was it all about? Some men, and not just *some* men, but some elegant, finely-dressed men with splendid careers going to a house and deciding to eat themselves to death!" Then Aron quotes from the film, and to G. it sounds as if he does so verbatim: *"If you don't eat, then you don't die."* Aron says he doesn't want to talk about it any more. But he continues regardless: "He's lying there with a bulging belly, and while another of them stuffs him further full of mashed potato, he tells them his mother forbade him . . ." He pauses here, possibly because the person he is talking to has interrupted him. "That she forbade him from doing so, ever since he was a small child," he adds. Aron is talking about the character Michel, but G. guesses that he is unwilling to plainly state the character's problem. "Why are we being shown something like that? Why would you, of all people, send someone to something like that? What's that? *My* mom? My dad, rather. You don't understand what his people are like. Yes, they're from São Paulo."

•

But despite the antipathy *La Grande bouffe* seems to have aroused in Aron's mind, it is clear that he is moved to discuss it further. And G. must admit to himself that he admires how artfully Aron manages to tiptoe his words around what most troubled him, how he sidles past saying directly that the pink-clad Michel's mother prevented him from breaking wind since childhood, that that suppression had gone on to cause his death. "It kills him!" Aron exclaims into the phone, and for a moment G. feels like the half-Brazilian actually feels compassion for the character in question. During the screening, Aron had plainly protested, if you interpret his "no" quite literally, when it was first made clear that Michel was in trouble because of his accumulated bloating, when he got up from the dinner table where they sat, the four gentlemen with the three prostitutes and the teacher Andrea, and went out onto the terrace and down to the gravel in front of the house, where he farted so loudly, and for so long, that he was forced to cover his ears, it was as if some kind of machine had been set in motion, like something was taking off. And when Andrea, a little later, just before the toilet erupted, sat on top of Michel, and the sounds from his body became aqueous and swelling, Aron had had enough, and voiced his feelings from his seat with such loud complaints that one of the other moviegoers got fed up with Aron's voluble commentary, echoing the way Aron had been annoyed with G. at the beginning of the movie. But, to be fair, Aron succeeded in making himself understood. The person shouting at Aron, on the other hand, had used such unintelligible words that G. felt sure neither Aron nor he could parse the words, even if their meaning was abundantly clear. G. ponders what kind of movies might suit Aron's taste, and what he had expected when his friend recommended the movie over the phone at the sports bar. He let himself stick around for roughly a hundred minutes, up until Michel's death scene; he was able to make it that far. G. realizes he is beginning to defend Aron. Had Aron been intelligible, and another patron not? Are men like Aron ever intelligible? If G. explained things to Aron, would they be intelligible to him?

•

He does not know what determines it, but almost as soon as Aron ends the conversation with his friend, G. goes over to the phone by the toilets in order to call Aron. He has watched him drink practically without pause from his pint glass and shot; it seems to have affected him, talking about his experience in the movie theater. Aron looks straight ahead, as if some emptiness in his eyes protects him from the other stimuli inside the bar. At no point has G. definitively seen Aron looking in his direction. He cannot see that he does so now, as he stands up and goes toward the restrooms. And when G. turns around, before he leaves the bar's main room, Aron is still looking dead ahead, a lonely sight. For a moment G. holds off on calling him, but he stifles his hesitation the very next moment. The phone on the wall works, as it should, when he feeds it change. G. thought such devices couldn't be found any longer. He calls directory services and asks for Aron Cesar's number. As when he called the same number earlier, he does not expect to need the last name. But when the girl on the end of the line claims to "have two Aron Cesars," G. adds his mother's name, and notes that there is only one S in it, and Cesar with a C. "A bank employee?" the girl asks. "A *banker*?" G. asks. "There are two Aron Cesar Óskarsons here," says the girl. "With a C." But then she says it's likely the same person in both cases, that Aron Cesar has probably registered twice. G. asks the girl to give him Aron's cellphone number and asks her again if indeed he is listed as being a banker. She tells him yes, and asks whether she can connect him, she uses the phrase *put you through*. He opts out; he will make the call.

·

A banker? Could that be? he wonders. Presumably, it is a joke on Aron's part. But who am I now, who will I be, when I call Aron? G. wonders. Someone other than the person who called him earlier today? As Aron answers, G. can hear the noise of the World Cup over the phone, but he feels like the rock music, which still seems to be coming from the same LP or CD as before, reaches him from the room but not over the phone. "Who's this?" Aron asks. "It's Eddi," says G. "Eddi?" "Where are you?" G. asks. "This isn't Eddi," Aron protests. "This is a different Eddi. Not the Eddi who talked to you this morning," G. says, himself surprised by where the idea comes from. And he adds: "I'm going to join you later." "What are you talking about?" Again G. thinks that Aron sounds like a teenager. "I'm going to come with you to Nóra's," he says. "Tell me who this is," Aron demands. "What's the address?" G. asks. "Did you call me earlier?" asks Aron; it is like his voice is growing up. "Who is this?" Who is whom? G. asks himself. Who said those words? "You told me to come if I wanted to," he says. Who? G. asks again. "Who the hell is this?!" shouts Aron. "Eddi. The same one who you spoke to this

morning. I called you for lunch when you were in the bookstore."
"What are you talking about? What makes you think I was in a
bookstore this morning?" "*She definitely won't mind,*" G. whispers,
adding in the same tone: "Will you be bringing something with
you?" "Who is this?" Aron repeats. "You know who this is." "No,
I don't." And involuntarily, like something in the surroundings
brings forth the words from his lips, G. lets out "*Quiet down back
there.*" He feels the need to piss, suddenly very urgent. "Who the
hell is this?" shouts Aron. "Michel," says G. Again silence for a
moment. "What are you talking about? Michel-what?" And G.
answers, "Marcello." "Tell me who you are," Aron says, and tries
to calm down. "Marcello Mastroianni," answers G. "Quit doing
this!" shouts Aron. "Tell me who this is! Who is this?" "Sara,"
replies G., then follows up with Sara's last name. Again silence
from Aron. They are both silent. Then Aron asks, "What are you
talking about? Sara who?" He pretends not to know her. "This
is Sara," reiterates G., and mentions her father's name, her last
name, again. "Sorry, but I don't know that person," says Aron. He
sounds deliberate and cold. This has thrown him off balance. "I
don't think this is funny anymore," he says. G. cannot wait any
longer to pee. He returns the receiver to the wall, and grabs the
handle of the toilet door, but decides first to peek out, curious
about Aron's reaction. He places himself behind the rectangular
support column, from which he can observe Aron from about
five meters away. And that brings to mind an image of Aron
at lunch, as he looked out of the window on Þingholtsstræti—
pale—which is how G. sees Aron now, pale. He watches him tap
a number into his phone, then wave to the bartender and signal

that he has an empty shot glass on his table. He then takes a sip of beer, and sets the phone to his ear. Despite the babble of voices inside the bar and the noise of the soccer, which seems to be noticeably louder than before, G. hears Aron ask into the phone "What's the listing for this number." If Aron had been pale a moment before, he goes white at the information the girl, possibly the same one G. spoke to, gives him. Or so G. imagines. But he also imagines that Aron doesn't know the public phone is by the toilets, that he must assume the phones in here are by the bar itself and inside the office. G.'s about to piss himself. He sees the bartender bringing an alcoholic morsel to Aron's table, and he hurries into the toilet. As he glances in the mirror over the sink a moment, he finds he can discern a smile in his eyes; he allows himself to move it to his lips. Then he lifts the toilet seat, and looks down into the gleaming white bowl. And pisses. He looks at his penis, this slouch who has never been anywhere, except down into his underwear and back up again. And he con- templates the yellow jet coming out of it.

•

Aron pretends not to know the name. He finds it uncomfort- able to hear. He argues that Sara does not exist. That she *has* not existed. G. tucks his penis back inside his underwear, zips up his fly, wipes a little urine from the side of the toilet bowl, flushes, and washes his hands.

•

But Aron isn't there when he comes back out. All three glasses on the table are empty, not even his outline remains, so abruptly has he left the place. And G. himself bids the bar goodbye, with the girl's voice in his mind, the one who taught him that Aron Cesar Óskarson had registered himself as a banker. Was that Sara? Is that where she's hiding, providing information about other people? Would she read aloud from the letter G. had sent her, if she was asked to do so?

•

The rain is not as heavy as before. G. looks down Frakkastígur, but there is no Aron. Could he have gone up to Laugavegur, or down to Hverfisgata? G., of course, has no idea how far up or down Barónsstígur Nóra lives. He guesses Aron chose Hverfisgata. When he reaches the corner and looks up the street without spotting Aron, he calls to mind that there is an Indian food joint in a building on the right; when he reaches the place he realizes that it is the same kind of place they disappeared into, the three bankers on Lækjargata. Perhaps their colleague, Aron, has headed inside? He looks in the window, seeing several customers at the counter, but Aron is not among them. Presumably he has lost him. He made a mistake going to the toilet inside the bar. But as he keeps on walking in the vague hope that Aron has paused along the way to smoke, at almost the next moment his wish is granted; it's as if he's been heard. When he comes around the corner of the corrugated iron building that houses the restaurant, he becomes aware of a person up against the wall, and in the nick of time, before the person becomes aware of him, G. manages to about-face, to hurry across the street to the other sidewalk, where he can hide behind a car. It is Aron standing by the wall, G. saw that immediately. He's smoking. He holds a cigarette a finger's length from his lips. He faces a large parking lot the size of three, maybe four house widths, and he notices that he has his left hand on his belly. He's frowning. He sets his shoulders and leans slightly forward, a pained expression on his face. He closes his eyes, throws away his cigarette, and puts both hands on his stomach. Then he turns his head away from the street, even more wracked by cramps. For a moment, it occurs to G. that perhaps he should be worried about Aron. But Aron suddenly stretches, and looks toward the street, seeming to feel comparatively better. G. stoops a trifle lower so the car covers him better. Aron fishes out another cigarette. After several puffs, he walks rapidly across the parking lot, and G. follows him along the other side of the street. They cross Vitastígur, and past several houses, until they come to another, bigger parking lot, larger than that by the Indian place. Aron heads across the lot, going diagonally toward Barónsstígur. Again he casts away a still-burning cigarette; it lands on a car. And G. sees him light yet one more, after he crosses Laugavegur, through an unusually packed crowd of people, a sign something special is happening in town. Something's going on. And he grafts those words on Aron and his journey, a journey that is probably near its end. Is he smoking all those cigarettes, because he knows they will be his last? G. can hear barking. Not just from one dog; at least two. He hears it coming from a backyard on the right side of Barónstígur, just past the corner with Laugavegur. And he thinks about the death on the balcony, the peace that followed the pitiful image of Michel on the railing. And he briefly thinks he's perceived something similar here on this street corner in downtown Reykjavík, something like a loud silence. This is how a city sounds, or is silent, when besieged.

•

Aron continues up Barónsstígur. He reaches the corner with Grettisgata, and pauses. G. stops too. He looks through the window of some kind of bookstore or gallery in the house down from the kiosk on the corner. And he notices that Aron has fixed his eyes on a particular house on this side of the street, further up. He takes out his phone and dials. He is asking for Nóra's house number, G. speculates. What's more, the call only lasts a few seconds. He waits by the storefront as Aron heads along the sidewalk on the other side, and does not start after him until he disappears into the alleyway about midway along the block between the corner and Bergþórugata. Aron has gone in by the time G. reaches the passageway. He creeps along the graffitied wall, and peeks around the corner to the right. He sees Aron standing on some kind of wooden platform, perhaps a balcony, knocking on a door, or maybe a window. There are many plants in the yard, and *Haus und Garten* surfaces in G's mind, the magazine Aron had flipped through in the bookstore, and *Interior Design*, too, the one G. himself had reached for. How long a period has passed since he followed Aron into the bookstore. He feels like their whole lifetimes lie between that moment and now, here in this courtyard off Barónstígur. But suddenly Aron disappears into the house, like he's being pulled inside. Did he throw away his cigarette? Did he want to set fire to the plants in the garden? Does he know that the rain has already extinguished the embers? G. walks along the fence that encloses the garden, and positions himself by a tall birch. The rain worsens. It's now as dark as it ever gets in an Icelandic summer. G. guesses that Nóra's apartment is framed by the three windows above the wooden platform. In the middle, there's a door, or rather a window that reaches down to the floor, and G. thinks it likely that the windows on either side belong to the living room and the bedroom, with the kitchen facing out to the street on the other side. Light yellow curtains are drawn across all the windows, and when G. tries to detect whether the door is closed he sees the shape of a tall person behind the pale, yellow fabric. Nóra. This is she. Nóra appears to have long hair. And she is thin. When she puts her hand to the door handle, as though to make sure it is actually locked, G. hears a loud shout from the window or door of another apartment in the vicinity. It seems to be coming from the next house. Could it be someone is that caught up in Greece versus Ivory Coast in the World Cup? Nóra has disappeared from the window-door. G. moves a little further along the fence, trying to catch sight of Aron inside the apartment, but it is Nóra who again lets herself be seen, although G. cannot see her very well. She is in the window to the left, setting a candlestick in the windowsill, putting a tall candle into the holder. Then she turns around, and seems to give Aron a sign to come to her; he, G., or she, rather, Nóra, only needs to wait a few moments before Aron's faint silhouette appears. He is no longer the stooping salesman crouching over the low living room table. He flicks on his lighter, and carries the candle over to the window. Then Nóra embraces him, and G. thinks he places his hands somewhere lower down, and they disappear from the window, over to the next, the window-door, then somewhere else, and he can't see them anymore. He tries to imagine how close the candle is to the window curtains. The flame illuminates them beautifully, but he can't see what colors lie behind the screen. He thinks it likely that the candle is white. But the flame will be blue, the type of fire that eats up paper.

Tomorrow

I believe I stand by the fence for five or six minutes after Aron lights the candle. But what am I thinking? Who? Who thinks what? Him? The one who has never been anywhere? He goes into the living room in Philippe's house in Paris. In off the balcony. And he moves things about on the piano so they are arranged the same way as the things, or the same kinds of things, that live on the piano in his parents' living room. The lamp with the light brown shade he puts on the right side, and the dark blue and white vase, the Chinese one, on the left. He then moves into his own living space in the basement. His blonde mat from Isfahan, which his father got permission from his mother for him to have, after a comment he made that the blonde—the mat, not the mother!—would enjoy the cellar better than being hidden inside their bedroom; he cannot decide whether the mat should be on the floor in front of the coffee table or on the wall above the Danish console. And because of this, the blonde mat lies on the floor. And he calls to mind the rim that formed when he brushed the dust from the chiffonier a few weeks ago. He calls it a rim, but he knows that another word would better fit the thick ridge that took shape after he stroked the orange dust cloth over this tall piece of furniture he had forgotten to wipe down for several years.

•

His gleaming furniture, safe in the secure custody of time. His things. Himself.

•

He fancies *crêpes suzette*, the pancakes Ugo and Marcello ate while they were sitting at Michel's feet, watching Andrea sit on top of him, pushing out of him dry, rasping sounds that then became by turns wet and foaming. But most of all he wants to see the film again; he cannot wait to see it again. And this time he will be better prepared for the final minutes. He still has not followed *the other* two gentlemen, Philippe and Ugo, to their deaths. It is Wednesday tomorrow. Nigeria and Argentina are facing off in Brazil around midday, followed by Honduras and

Switzerland in the evening. He saw it in the paper in the super-market on Austurstræti.

•

He goes back the same way. Diagonally across the large car park, and over Vitastígur and Frakkastígur, where several noisy men are standing outside the rock bar and smoking, no doubt discussing the course of events in the game. He comes up to the empty movie theater box office. The boy who sold him the ticket has moved over to the concessions stand, and tells him that the film is on the schedule for tomorrow. The same time as today.

•

It is not until he reaches the corner of Laugavegur and Vatns-stígur that he realizes what he saw. Or *whom*. It was past Hver-fisgata, on the lower part of Vatnsstígur, where Vatnsstígur meets Veghúsastígur. He turns around and looks back down the street. Where is he now? He is hiding. But he is not exactly in camou-flage; he has slipped up. He knows about him. Perhaps the color of his pants and outerwear, the so-called reporter's jacket, has disappeared into the gray that covers the evening, but G. knows he is wearing a hat, the movie theater baseball cap, in colors that would never try to hide, were they alive and had they an inde-pendent will. And when he scans for him, in the knowledge that he is there somewhere, G. feels how good it is to have someone concerning themselves with what you do, or where you go.

•

He has never felt as good as now, under the raised umbrella. As he walks down the street, and the rain on the stretched nylon makes him feel like he is indoors, he hears a tune from *La Grande bouffe*, the refrain he imagines was composed especially for the film. He hums it first the way Michel played it on the piano. Michel had then sped up, and finally let it run away from itself. He then added on top the orchestral arrangement, the way it sounds on the record they put on the phonograph in the living room. That version offered more of a chance to dance than the piano version. And they danced to the song, Philippe and the teacher, Andrea. It was a chaste dance, the way I think dancing should be.

•

I look forward to getting home. I'm going to remember to look up who it was who wrote the poem about the days being full. It's called "Waking Up." I remember it. Getting to one's feet. It focuses on the act of composition. Writing. That one has no time to lose, that one must hasten to phrase things anew, or to have them represent something different. I have reached the pharmacy where I bought the cream. Several foreign tourists stand in a knot under their umbrellas in front of the Danish store on the other side of the street, and I slow down a bit in my stride so I can attempt to hear them. They are speaking Italian. To hear how the words end, which is so completely unlike how words in my own language end, causes me to look forward even more to getting home to Aragata, though I do not know why. I sense even better than before the proximity of the blue man behind me; I know he paused at the window of the bookstore on the corner before the pharmacy when I slowed down to hear the Italian. I cannot wait to get through the door to my house, and know that Mom can hear I'm home. She will call down to me, on the home phone, to let me know Dad is still asleep. Or dead. And I am going to allow myself to light the candle that I have placed in the candle-holder on the smoking table. And put Jaroussky on my music player, his *Opium* recordings, and try to hear how the forthcoming version of the Verlaine poem by the contra-tenor and the Ebène Quartet will sound, the one I read about in the magazine at noon. But before I light the candle, I am going to bring my mother the cream, and ask her to give me the letter she wants me to mail for her. Because I am going to go back there tomorrow, with the envelope containing the manuscript, before I go to the movie theater. And it, the manuscript, will be unchanged from this morning. I had been deliberating over the title I'd given it—for a brief moment I felt that *The Dandy* might suit the story better, especially with a view to rewarding Aron Cesar for having had the idea of calling someone by that name, but I've decided to stick with the original title.

B ragi Ólafsson is the author of several books of poetry and short stories, along with six novels, including *The Pets* and *The Ambassador*, both
of which are available from Open Letter Books. He is also a former bass
player with The Sugarcubes, the internationally successful pop group that
featured Björk as the lead vocalist.

Lytton Smith is a poet, professor, and translator from the Icelandic. His most recent translations include works by Kristin Ómarsdóttir, Jón Gnarr, Ófeigur Sigurðsson, and Guðbergur Bergsson.

**OPEN
LETTER**

**OPEN
LETTER**